TEKNET

WILLIAM SHATNER

ACE BOOKS, NEW YORK

This Ace Book contains the complete text of the original
hardcover edition. It has been completely reset in a typeface
designed for easy reading, and was printed from new film.

TEK NET

An Ace Book / published by arrangement with
the author

PRINTING HISTORY
Ace/Putnam hardcover edition / 1997
Ace mass-market edition / March 1999

The Penguin Putnam Inc. World Wide Web site address is
http://www.penguinputnam.com

For further information about William Shatner and his other literary
works, check out his World Wide Web site at
http://www.williamshatner.com

ISBN: 0-441-00604-3

ACE®
Ace Books are published
by The Berkley Publishing Group,
a member of Penguin Putnam Inc.,
375 Hudson Street, New York, New York 10014.
ACE and the "A" design are trademarks
belonging to Charter Communications, Inc.

PRINTED IN THE UNITED STATES OF AMERICA

10 9 8 7 6 5 4 3 2 1

This seems to be the last of the Tek books. It's been a long run and a good run. I've dedicated the many previous books to various people who had a lot or at least something to do with the success of the series. I'd like to dedicate this last book to people who had nothing whatsoever to do with this endeavor.

My sisters, Joy and Farla, have had absolutely nothing to do with this book. My wonderful assistant, Stephanie Riggs, who is both cool and beautiful, has had nothing to do with this book. And my ex-wife has had nothing to do with this book except to get half the proceeds. But most of all, I'd like to dedicate this book to Martika and Stirling, who, as dogs, could not have written a word, but their bark is worse than their bite. I can't say the same for Ron Goulart; my agent, Carmen LaVia; and my editor, Susan Allison, all of whom absolutely had a great deal to do with this book.

TEKNET

1

JUST BEFORE THEY caught up with her on the grounds of the Hollywood Starwalk Park that night—less than five minutes before, actually—she made the call.

Not to her current husband, or her current lover.

On that chilly, foggy evening in the late spring of the year 2122, Jill Bernardino vidphoned Sid Gomez. She hadn't seen him or even talked to him in over three years, but she felt he was one of the few people in all of Greater Los Angeles who could help her.

A dark-haired woman in her late thirties, Jill wasn't quite ready to turn to the SoCal Police. She had a couple of good reasons.

"But maybe I'll have to anyway," she told herself as she made her way, cautiously and uneasily, along the quirky, seemingly tree-lined passways of the mist-shrouded and nearly deserted park.

She'd initially expected to meet someone here tonight. An informant, a man who could supply her with information for the vidwall movie she was working on.

"Not so," she'd realized a few moments ago.

This was a setup, just something to lure her here.

"So, obviously, somebody knows about what I know."

Suddenly off to her right a row of holographic palm trees began sputtering. The noise made Jill flinch and dodge to her left, shivering.

The tall trees, over a dozen of them, crackled and vanished. The fog took their place.

Up ahead, beneath a large floating litesign that urged *Walk Thru Movieland's Past*, stood three rusty androids. They represented famed Hollywood movie stars from an earlier century. The only one Jill recognized was, she was nearly certain, Clark Gable.

The andy was in need of repairs and the lazy salute he gave her as she approached was jerky. His grin was more a grimace and it locked into place and wouldn't fade. "Welcome to bygone Hollywood, sweetheart," he told her in a rattling, raspy voice.

When the blonde actress on Gable's left winked at Jill, her plastiglass eyeball fell out. It hit the simulated white gravel of the path and bounced once. "Hiya, kiddo."

The third mechanical actor, a lanky cowboy, lifted his pearl-white Stetson, bowing to the unknown blonde. He bent to retrieve the eyeball. "Allow me, ma'am."

Losing his balance in the process, the long, lean cowboy fell flat out on the ground. His long legs twitched a few times and then he was still and the night fog came rolling in over him.

Jill hurried on, glancing back.

She was certain she was being followed. Back there in the thickening fog, there were at least two people on her trail. She'd caught glimpses of them in the swirling mist. A small, bald man and a larger, broader figure.

"Might be an andy, that second one."

Jill increased her pace, then went running up the steps

of what looked to be an old Southern mansion from several centuries ago. Another Clark Gable was there on the wide verandah, dressed as some kind of Southern gentleman this time. This android wasn't quite as weather-worn and his grin was warmer.

"Good evening, my dear," he greeted, tipping his Mississippi gambler's hat.

She pushed through the door, shut it behind her and found herself in an immense drawing room. Some of the simulated furniture was flickering and more than one of the hidden holoprojectors was making odd humming sounds.

Crouching behind an ornate love seat, Jill yanked her palmphone out of her jacket pocket and, hurriedly, punched out Gomez' number.

The curly-haired detective's smiling face popped up on the tiny screen after the third buzz. "*Buenas noches*," he said.

"Sid, listen—I'm in danger."

He recognized her now, frowning. "You've got the wrong *hombre*, Jill. I'm your *erstwhile* husband," he told her. "Erstwhile, a word often misused, means former. I no longer—"

"For Christ sake, knock off the whimsy and listen to me," his ex-wife pleaded. "I'm in the old run-down Hollywood Starwalk Park—you know, near where the Hollywood Bowl used to be. You've got to—"

"If one of your multitude of beaus has abandoned you, *chiquita*, I advise you to phone a skycab and—"

"Let's save time," she cut in. "During the two and a half some years we were married, I was a Tekhead and I did fool around. Right now though, Sid, I swear, I think I'm in serious trouble."

His frown deepened. "Okay, what sort of trouble?"

"I'm not completely sure," she told him, glancing toward the door. "I'm back writing again, Sid, working on a vidwall movie. It's a thriller called *Hokori*, and—"

"An entire movie about the late and sleazy Teklord?"

"Yes, but the point is—well, while researching the damn thing I came across something. Some information and—Sid, get here quickly. I'm sure I was lured to this dump. A couple of goons are trailing me."

"Got any kind of gun?"

"No, I hate weapons and—"

"I'll be over there in ten minutes. Meantime, call the cops."

"The local police still don't trust me because of all the trouble I used to get into when I was a Tekkie, Sid. I—"

"Call 'em nonetheless, *cara*," he urged her.

"Sid, okay, I will," she promised. "I'm in that imitation of the—I think it's the mansion from an ancient movie called *Gone With the Wind*. And listen, this has to do with a plan to . . ."

She stopped talking then.

The door of the colorful old Southern mansion had started to swing open.

═2═

GOMEZ' SKYCAR CAME swooping down through the thick fog to make a bouncy landing in the empty parking lot next to the ramshackle Hollywood Starwalk Park.

"This isn't the first dump like this I've had to drag her out of," he said as he stepped out into the chilly, swirling mist.

He went running across the damp rutted surface of the landing area.

"Never thought I'd be doing it again. Jill was . . . Whoa, *bastante*, enough," he told himself. "She's not your wife anymore so you can skip the self-pity, *amigo*."

Sprawled flat on his back just outside the open, weather-worn plazmetal gate was the android Charlie Chaplin who'd long ago served as ticket taker.

Skirting the fallen comedian, Gomez eased out his stun-gun from its shoulder holster. He began to jog along a wide weedy passway.

Back in the days when he was a SoCal State cop, he'd visited this place a lot, unofficially. He still remembered where the old Southern mansion was located.

He halted, turning to stare into the swirling mist at his left.

Nodding, he moved on. The figure he'd spotted looming over there was only an android, a defunct replica of a dark-clad werewolf from some forgotten motion picture of another century.

A moment later Gomez became aware of arguing voices up ahead on his right.

"We only got one goddamn Tek chip, asshole," a teenage girl was saying in a thin nasal voice. "And you dorfs promised me first turn."

There were three of them, the skinny girl and two lean young men, huddled on the porch of a rickety log cabin. They were fighting for the possession of a battered Tek Brainbox.

Slumped in the doorway of the cabin was an android Abe Lincoln, stovepipe hat tilted far down over his craggy forehead. A plump grey rat was sitting placidly in the andy's narrow lap.

The girl gave the Brainbox a violent tug, but didn't manage to get it away from the others. She was red-haired and there were several green and crimson snakes tattooed on her pale bare arms.

The larger of the youths said, "Let go, Snooky." His right hand flashed out, hit her, hard, across the face.

She let go of the box, stumbled and fell backwards. She landed directly in Gomez' path.

He crouched and, keeping his eye on the two youthful louts, aided the skinny girl to rise. "Usually, *pendejo*," he said in the direction of the one who'd slapped the girl down, "I'm noted as a gentle and patient teacher of morals and manners. Tonight, unfortunately, I'm in a hurry and this will have to suffice as your lesson in deportment."

Gomez aimed the stungun and fired.

The sizzling beam hit the young man in his narrow chest. He went rising up on his tiptoes. The Brainbox he was clutching dropped from his splayed fingers.

As the lout toppled over backwards to sit beside Lincoln and scare the rat into flight, Gomez continued on his way.

"Thanks, greaser," called the redhead. "Now I'll get my turn ahead of this pissant."

"*De nada*," he muttered, turning onto a side path that would lead him to the *Gone With the Wind* mansion where his former wife had been when she phoned him for help.

And she really was a former wife, he realized as he hurried along through the foggy night. Jill had been his second wife and he was now living with . . . either the fourth or fifth one. Sometimes, especially when he hadn't had enough sleep, he tended to lose track of how many there'd been.

"*Muy bonita* Jill was," he recalled. "Also very bright and talented. *Ai*, if only I'd been able to do something about her fondness for Tek—and for other *hombres*."

He slowed when he caught his first glimpse of the tumble-down mansion through the mist.

Leaving the path, he cut across a field that in better days had represented a trench-filled stretch of World War I battlefield.

Crouched low, Gomez moved closer to the looming house.

He approached the place from its left side. There was no light showing, no sound coming from within.

Up close to the white neowood wall, Gomez inched a handheld eavesdropper from his jacket pocket and, gently, touched it to the mansion's side.

The tiny dials indicated no human inhabitants.

Circling around to the front, he climbed the stairs openly.

The Clark Gable android nodded. "Welcome, sir," he

said. "You look like a true Southern gentleman."

"*Sí*, but from a little farther south than you mean," replied the detective, crossing the threshold into a shadowy hallway.

In the large drawing room he found a palmphone lying on the threadbare carpet. "This has got to be hers," he said, not touching it.

From another pocket he extracted a small gadget, this one called a sniffer.

Activating it, Gomez did a slow, careful sweep of the whole room.

After seven minutes the sniffer's tiny voxbox told him, "A female of about forty years was here within the past hour."

"*Sí*—and?"

"One human and a robot entered approximately five minutes later," continued the reedy metallic voice. "There was a struggle."

"What sort of a struggle, *niño*?"

"A brief one. The woman was rendered unconscious—most probably by means of a stungun. Then she was taken from here."

"*Gracias*." Turning off the gadget, Gomez returned it to his pocket and glanced around the room. "*Bueno*—that means Jill was alive when she left this joint."

Spotting a chair that was real and not a holographic projection, he sat down, leaned back and let out a long, slow sigh.

"But there's no way of telling if she's still alive." He rubbed his hand over the lower half of his face, shaking his head. "This is a rough one, I'm afraid. Yeah, it smells *muy malo* to me."

He fetched out his own palmphone and punched out a number.

"Well, I'm going to have to find her," he said. "And I'll need Jake to help me."

Above the fog that was drifting in across the night Pacific the sky was a sharp, clear black. Jake Cardigan, fifty and good-looking in a been-around sort of way, was piloting the skycar on its return trip from the San Diego Sector of Greater LA.

Bev Kendricks, a pretty blonde woman, was in the passenger seat, leaning back and gazing up through the viewpanel in the cabin ceiling. "What'd you think?" she asked him.

Several seconds later Jake responded. "About the concert?"

"That—or anything else."

He shrugged his right shoulder. "Technically it was okay, but I guess I prefer live musicians to androids."

"Be difficult to see Duke Ellington's orchestra live."

"True."

After a silence, Bev said, "I'm going to say something, Jake."

"Sounds ominous."

She continued, "We have quite a lot in common. You've spent most of your grown-up life in law enforcement and so have I. You're a damned good private investigator now and so am I."

"A better private eye than I am," he told her.

"We've been together a lot in the past year or so." Frowning, he glanced over at her. "This is starting to sound like a farewell address."

Bev gave a slow sigh. "I like you a hell of a lot, Jake. But . . ."

"But?"

She moved a hand back and forth in front of her face,

as though she were brushing away cobwebs or mist. "I've mentioned this before and I don't mean to nag," said Bev. "But it hasn't gotten any better. Fact is, you seem, much too often, to be very depressed."

"Really? I see myself as being nothing short of jolly lately."

Bev inhaled slowly before speaking again. "I know how much you loved Beth Kittridge. I understand how hard her death hit you."

"That's the trouble, huh? To you it seems I'm still in mourning for her."

"She was killed quite a while ago by the Teklords and— Christ, Jake, the other night in bed you actually called me Beth."

"You should have told me then. I'm sorry."

"You should see somebody, talk about this," suggested Bev. "I know the Cosmos Detective Agency has a better maxmed plan than even my agency. So you could easily—"

"Nope, no. I have to work this all out on my own."

She shook her head. "I don't think you can."

Looking straight ahead into the dark night, Jake said, "You probably already know this. I'm not trying to hurt you. But in my life so far I've only really loved two women."

"I know, yes. And neither one is me."

"My wife Kate was the first." His voice was low, far away. "She was—like nobody I'd even met up until then. Of course, it turned out to be like a Tek dream that I conjured up for myself without needing a chip or a Brainbox."

"You don't have to tell me about Kate. I already know about her." Bev reached over and put her hand on his.

"I talk about it to remind myself how stupid and naïve I used to be," Jake said. "I never had a single damned doubt about Kate. Shit—and she helped the Sonny Hokori Tek Cartel set me up and she slept with . . ." He wasn't able to finish the sentence.

"That's the past, Jake. It's gone."

"No, it's a place I can visit anytime I want," he said. "Hell, I even end up there when I don't want to go."

The voxbox on the control dash spoke. "Emergency call from Sid Gomez."

Jake said, "I'll take it."

The small rectangular screen came to life and there was Gomez looking uneasy and downcast. "This isn't agency business, *amigo*," he began, "but I need your help."

"Tell me," invited Jake.

His partner said, "You remember my second wife, don't you?"

"Jill Bernardino, sure."

"Okay, I got a call from her about an hour or so ago," continued Gomez. "Jill told me she was down here at the Hollywood Starwalk Park and was afraid she was being trailed by some goons."

"She contacted you instead of the cops?"

"I'll explain that later," Gomez said. "Important thing is that Jill's gone. It looks like she was tagged and abducted."

"Any idea why?"

Gomez answered, "She's back writing, working on a vidwall movie about our old Tek chum, the late Sonny Hokori."

"That bastard," said Jake. "You figure there's a Tek angle to her kidnapping?"

"I think, Jake, that in the course of her researches she found out something she wasn't supposed to find out."

"But Hokori's outfit is completely defunct. We took care of most of that."

"We can speculate at length later," suggested his partner. "Can you get down here?"

"Within a half hour," Jake assured him.

— 3 —

JAKE PACED THE large drawing room, hands in pockets. "Okay, give me the rest of what you've got."

Gomez was sitting on the edge of an armchair, holding a palm-size e-notebook. "Jill arrived here by way of a sky-cab," he told his partner. "It picked her up at an address over in the Laguna Sector of Greater LA. That turns out to be her present home."

"Robot cabbie?"

"*Sí*, and the bot claims nobody tailed them and nothing else unusual occurred."

"What about other cabs that deposited people in the vicinity?"

"Nobody was brought to within a block of this ruin since early this morning," answered Gomez. "I doubt those two *cabrones* lurked around here that long."

Jake stopped pacing and straddled a straight-back chair. "You mentioned she was working on a script about the late, lamented Sonny Hokori."

"The same Tek entrepreneur who helped frame you into

a stay up in the Freezer.'' He pointed at the ceiling with his thumb.

"Sonny's dead and gone, so's his sister," said Jake thoughtfully. "But there are still a lot of other Teklords above the ground."

"I don't know exactly what Jill found out, but it was sufficient to get her snatched."

"We ought to be able to gather some facts from one of our informants."

"You want to handle that angle, *amigo*?" Gomez stood up, clicked off the e-notebook and slipped it into a side pocket.

"While you?"

"First off I'm going to visit her *hacienda* and talk to her current husband," replied the detective. "He's a gent named Ernst Reinman."

"Which husband is this by now?"

Gomez held up four fingers. "*Cuatro*. I have the distinction of being the first in the series," he said. "She's been hooked up with this Reinman for a bit over two years and he's an executive with a charitable org called the Starvation Center."

"During her days with you," mentioned Jake, "she had a tendency to stray now and then. Would there currently be other gentlemen friends in her life?"

"I've already got somebody researching that for me," Gomez said. "But I do know that a gent by the name of Mervyn Illsworth has been providing Jill with some of her background information for the script."

"I'll check on him before I contact any informants," volunteered Jake.

"Illsworth resides at Tube Village in the Long Beach Sector."

Jake then inquired, "And why didn't Jill want to bring the police in on this?"

"Mostly, far as I know, because she used to have a rotten reputation with the SoCal law and still likes to avoid them as much as possible," said Gomez. "During her heyday as an enthusiastic Tek customer—well, she got in several fairly serious tangles with the forces of law and order."

Jake rose up. "Even so, Sid," he said, "if we don't find some trace of her within the next few hours—we have to bring them in."

"Agreed. Besides, once her hubby finds out she's among the missing, he'll more than likely do that himself."

"What about the Cosmos Agency?"

"I want to talk to our esteemed chief, Walt Bascom, about this whole business *mañana*," said Gomez. "If one or more of the big Tek cartels are planning some new deviltry—then our *jefe* ought to be able to sell that news to some of his many government agency contacts."

"My thought exactly," said Jake.

The night fog hung heavy over the two-acre stretch of simulated beach. Most of the sand was real, but the clusters of large black rocks and the scatters of seaweed and driftwood were all holographic projections.

An actual seagull was dozing beside a twisted, seemingly sea-worn chunk of wood. He made an annoyed sound, unfurled and then refolded his wings, as Jake passed him on foot on his way to one of the entry kiosks to the underground Tube City.

Kiosk 7 was manned by a pair of gunmetal guardbots. "Welcome to Tube City, sir," greeted the one with A25 stenciled in white across his wide chest. "You are?"

"Jake Cardigan," he answered. "I have an appointment with Mervyn Illsworth, who lives down on Level 5."

The second bot—F14 was his name—opened a panel in his metal chest. "While my colleague is taking you through the identification routine, sir," he said, "let me show you some of the popular Tube City souvenirs that are available at extremely reasonable prices."

"Actually, I'm trying," Jake informed him, "to free my life of any and all clutter."

F14 had a fairly large shelved compartment built into his upper torso. "Here you see," he announced, pointing into himself, "our very popular Tube City nearcaf mug, the equally popular Tube City cap, the Tube City plazshirt and—"

"If you'll hand me your ID packet, sir," requested A25. Jake obliged.

"You'll notice," went on F14, "that all our sought-after Tube City souvenirs have an appealing likeness of the famous Tube City mascot, Lowell the Mole, emblazoned on them."

"Cute little rascal," remarked Jake as he took back his identification materials. "Can I descend now?"

Nodding, A25 gestured at the grey floor. "Take the ramp to Entry Tube 7, sir," he instructed. "Then follow the lite-arrows down to Level 5. You'll find Mr. Illsworth residing in Section 5-N."

A portion of the floor came sliding open and Jake saw a brightly illuminated ramp slanting downward. "Thanks."

"We're having a two-for-one sale on the mugs," called F14 as Jake started down.

Mervyn Illsworth was very fat. Seeing him magnified to twice his actual size up on the high, wide vidwall made his bulk all the more impressive. "I appreciate, truly, your going along with this little quirk of mine, Cardigan," he was saying in his chirpy voice.

Jake was straddling a chair in the foyer of the researcher's underground apartment, after having made his way down through a succession of snaking tubes and tunnels. "I'm more interested in getting information than in seeing you face-to-face," he informed the fat man's image.

"I'm not exactly, you must understand, really a complete and total recluse," explained Illsworth. "Yet, I readily admit, I feel much more at ease if I remain here, snug in my studio, and visitors stay out there and we communicate electronically." The fat man was sprawled in a large, sturdy metal chair surrounded by keyboards and monitor screens.

"Okay, fine," said Jake, impatient. "Now what about Jill Bernardino?"

"I was, really, extremely upset when you phoned to inform me that Jill may've been kidnapped tonight, Cardigan," Illsworth said in his small, high-pitched voice. "Particularly if it might have something to do with information that I supplied her."

Jake asked, "Would she come here to your place?"

"Yes, frequently. I consider her, truly, a dear friend as well as a valued client," answered the fat man. "Jill, of course, always remained out there where you are."

"When did you talk to her last?"

"She dropped down here just yesterday afternoon to discuss some of the new material I'd unearthed relating to Sonny Hokori and his Tek activities. By the way, I'd very much like to interview you someday soon, Cardigan, about how the late Sonny attempted to destroy you and frame—"

"Let's get back to Jill," cut in Jake as he stood up and moved close to the giant image on the wall. "Did she mention being worried or talk about something she'd discovered in the course of her digging into the history of the Hokori Tek operations?"

Illsworth shook his massive head. "No, there was nothing like that, Cardigan,'' he answered. ''She did seem a bit depressed, but . . .''

''Well, what?''

''Oh, it occurs to me that Jill did make a rather odd remark yesterday,'' said the fat man. ''She and I were, as I've explained, dear buddies and sometimes we'd just talk about our personal lives and problems.''

''She was seeing somebody?''

The researcher's immense body quivered when he sighed. ''You know, then, about her unfortunate habit?''

''She tends to sleep around, yeah.''

''Can't help it really.'' Illsworth sighed once more. ''At any rate—Jill made this remark. She said something along the lines of, 'Maybe I didn't need you after all, Merv dear. I've just now found out I've been involved with somebody who knows more about this whole damn business than you do.' ''

''Who would that be?''

''I really haven't even a vague idea.''

''Didn't she confide the names of her boyfriends?''

''Not actually, no. She'd simply say, 'I saw the professor again last night,' or, 'I think it's time to drop the artist.' ''

''Are those actual designations—there really was a professor and an artist?''

Illsworth gave a jiggling affirmative nod. ''Yes, but I believe she did jettison the artist, whoever the devil he is, over three weeks ago,'' he piped. ''The professor, she was still seeing on the sly.''

''You don't know which of these guys has a possible Tek link?''

''No, I don't,'' he said apologetically. ''With most of the research I do, while it's not always orthodox and strictly kosher, I try not to do anything that'll annoy active crooks and criminals. However, if Jill continues missing—well, I intend to do some very intrusive digging.''

"You come up with anything, contact me at the Cosmos Detective Agency,'' requested Jake.

"I will,'' promised the fat man. "You don't, do you, suspect that the poor dear might already be dead?''

"That's just one,'' answered Jake, "of several unpleasant possibilities.''

—=4=—

THE HUGE LITESIGN that floated above the bright-lit pastel blue dome-restaurant proclaimed: *The Kafeteria Welcomes the Friends of the Starvation Center!*

Gomez went striding up the wide, slanting pastel pink ramp to the high arched entryway of the huge Altadena Sector restaurant.

Just inside the large crowded lobby a beautiful blonde young woman in a skin-tone sinsilk gown beckoned to him. "Where the bloody hell do you think you're going, Pancho?" she inquired in a throaty voice.

"Beg pardon?"

"You're not on the guest list for this fund-raising dinner," she informed him.

"That's absolutely true, *chiquita*. Nevertheless, I—"

"Please, don't toss any of those awful Mex expressions at me."

He gave her a very quick bow. "Forgive me," he said. "Now would you fill me in as to just what your official capacity is at this shindig?"

"It's none of your goddamn business, Pancho," she told

21

him. "Take flight now before I summon a couple of husky white men to toss you out on your Latino keester."

Gomez smiled at her. "My friends and associates now and then chide me for being too thin-skinned and sensitive," he said. "But, so help me, I think I sense some sort of ethnic undertones in our otherwise delightful conversation."

The blonde's nose wrinkled. "If there's one thing I dislike more than a Latino, it's a wiseass Latino."

"I thought it was the mission of the Starvation Center to feed the downtrodden—no matter what their nationality."

"Are you kidding? We limit ourselves to the passable races."

"Well, let's get on to the business at hand," he suggested. "I was informed at his residence that Ernst Reinman was here this evening."

"He's the keynote speaker, dumbbell."

"I have to talk to him."

"So you can hit him for the loan of a few pesos?"

"So I can discuss his wife with him."

The blonde took a step back from him. "Don't tell me you're another one of dear Jill's sackmates?"

"Go tell Reinman his wife appears to have been abducted," said Gomez evenly. "I'm an operative with the Cosmos Detective Agency."

"Oh, Lord," she gasped. "You're not just saying this because you think I was rude to you?"

"*Señora*, I don't care a fig for what you think of me or the land of my ancestors," he explained. "But I'm interested in finding Jill Bernardino. It may help if I talk to her husband."

She reached out, tentatively and cautiously, to pat the

detective on the arm. "You stay right here," she instructed. "I'll go get Ernst."

The kitchen staff consisted entirely of robots, at least ten of them, white-painted and wearing high white chef's caps. The big white room was thick with steam and the smells of cooking.

In a corridor just outside the open doorway Gomez and Ernst Reinman stood facing each other. "So," the detective was saying, "do you have any idea what—"

"Why did she call you and not me?" Reinman was a tall, heavyset man in his late fifties. He had a sad, weary face and was suffering from some sort of respiratory problem. "I am, after all, Jill's husband and you'd expect she'd turn to me when she's in trouble."

"She probably picked me because I'm a private investigator and she was about to have trouble with some dangerous criminal types."

"You're Gomez!" It sounded like an accusation.

"As I already mentioned when I introduced myself."

"Yes, but I only just now realized that you're *that* Gomez." Reinman paused to take a wheezing breath. "You were married to my wife."

"A long time ago," he acknowledged. "The point is, I think she's been kidnapped and if you have any idea as to who might have—"

"She's told me a lot about you, how you ruined the marriage with your philandering," said Jill's husband. "No, you're not an especially moral man, Gomez."

"I'm a rascal," he conceded. "Now let's get back to who would want to carry her off."

"Where'd you say this happened?"

"At the old Hollywood Starwalk Park in the Hollywood

Sector of GLA. Did your wife tell you who she was planning to meet there?''

Shaking his head, breathing shallowly, Reinman answered, ''I thought she was going to a class in ceramics at the University of California/Venice Sector Campus tonight. I have no idea why she would have visited that run-down old park.''

''She thought she was going to meet someone with important information on the movie script she was doing on Sonny Hokori.''

''That's not like her,'' said her husband. ''Jill's always been open and honest with me—that's one of the best things about our marriage.''

Gomez turned away, watching a robot dice vegetables. ''She didn't talk about the project with you? Say anything about this new source of background material?''

Reinman coughed, shaking his head again. ''What do the police think about all this, Gomez?''

''We haven't contacted them yet,'' he told the husband. ''I was hoping to find out a little more about what exactly Jill's tangled up with before—''

''Are you insane, man?'' cut in the angry Reinman. ''The SoCal State cops are the ones who can find my wife. You quit playing detective, damn you—this is far too important for that.'' He backed to the wall, braced himself against it with one hand, concentrated on his breathing for a moment. ''Yes, she told me about your partner, too. Cardigan, isn't it? A convicted Tekhead—a man who tried to get my wife to try that rotten stuff back when she was married to you.''

Gomez persisted. ''Have there been any unusual calls the past few days?''

''Nothing like that, no,'' Reinman replied. ''Well, there were a couple of somewhat odd messages from a small bald man who claimed to be a scriptwriter, too. He struck me as—No, I'm not going to play detective with you, Gomez, damn you!''

''By the time the cops—''

''I've got to phone them right now.'' Pushing free of the wall, Reinman walked rapidly away from Gomez. ''I imagine the law will be very much interested in talking to you, my friend.''

Gomez shook his head. ''Maybe I ought to take a brush-up course in interrogation,'' he said, and took his leave.

— 5 —

A SILVER LANDCYCLE came rushing along the Santa Monica Sector beach bike path. It burst out of the thick midnight fog, shimmied to a stop a few feet from the decorative palm tree Jake was waiting beneath.

A lean young Chinese hopped off the passenger seat. "Thanks, Nanette," he said as the cycle and its driver went chuffing swiftly away into the heavy mist. He smoothed the long overcoat he was wearing, then smiled over at Jake. "Glad we're doing some business again, chum."

Jake said, "Once I heard you were back in SoCal, Timecheck, I immediately put you at the top of my list of trusted paid informants."

The Chinese left the path, pausing on the sand. He rolled up the right sleeve of his overcoat, revealing a silver-plated arm that had fifteen clock faces embedded in it. "Sorry I'm two minutes and seventeen seconds late, Jake," the informant apologized. "My ladyfriend dawdled over her nearcaf. She's a great-looking woman, don't you think?"

"Stunning. What have you found out for me?"

The lean young man was scowling at his cyborg arm.

Bringing it up close to his face, he rubbed away some of the night mist with his flesh hand. "Damn, Paris time is off eleven point five seconds again. Hell."

"Jill Bernardino," reminded Jake.

Reluctantly, Timecheck rolled the sleeve down over all the watches and joined Jake beneath the tree. "She's in considerable trouble."

"I already know that."

The two of them began to walk along the sand. "What you don't know, however, is that a consortium of very powerful European-based Tek cartels ordered her to be grabbed."

"Right, I didn't know that. Which Teklords are we talking about?"

"Those details I haven't found out yet," admitted Timecheck. He suddenly halted, frowned, scowled, rolled up his sleeve. "Yeah, just as I suspected. My Tokyo timepiece has stopped ticking." He tapped the dial with the tip of his finger.

"Try to learn exactly which cartels are involved."

"An extra five hundred dollars that'll cost, chum."

"An extra three hundred."

"I'm starting to think I'm going to have to take the arm in for an overhaul." He rolled down his sleeve and they started walking again. "Being as we're old buddies, Jake, and have done business in various odd corners of this giddy globe, I'll find out—probably at great personal risk to myself—just which Teklords are behind this caper, for a mere three hundred and fifty."

Jake nodded acceptance of the fee. "Who snatched her from the park?"

"I'm tracing that now. You'll get the news soon as it comes in," answered the informant. "When you're dealing with Tek cartels, you have to be extra sly and sneaky."

"Got anything on where they took her or what they intend to do with her?"

"That's another thing that remains to be found out, buddy."

After a few silent seconds Jake asked, "When several powerful Tek organizations get together it means something unusual is going on. So what's afoot, Timecheck?"

"You don't want to know."

"Meaning?"

"I haven't anything specific," said Timecheck. "But I'm getting hints that there's a very big deal underway."

"And Jill Bernardino found out about it?"

"That would be my conclusion, sure."

The fog was getting even thicker, closing in tighter around them as they walked.

Jake said, "What about her personal life?"

Timecheck chuckled, blowing on his metal fingers. "She's a very restless lady," he observed. "The artist you heard she was fooling with isn't exactly an artist. But I'm near certain it has to be a fellow named Ogden Vargas who builds robot puppets that he uses in making vidwall commercials."

"And her professor friend?"

"Easy, he's with UC/Venice. Jeffrey Monkwood. Thirty-five, overweight by twenty-some pounds, teaches in the Advanced Communications Department. Our Jill's been keeping company with him for the past three and a half months. Her husband has been led to believe she's studying ceramics, which is a new name for shacking up."

"You've got addresses on these guys?"

"Hey, Jake, this is Timecheck you're dealing with here," he reminded. "I'm a full-service stool pigeon. All the data is already reposing in both your home computer and your skycar infofile."

"Anything else to pass along?"

Timecheck said, "Only other thing I can pass along is some useful advice, which is yours absolutely free," he said. "Whatever you do—don't do a damn thing that'll annoy these Teklords."

"I already figured that out on my own," Jake told him.

The pretty blonde android waitress at the AllNite Neptune Café had been delivered only yesterday and she still had that new-appliance scent clinging to her. "What'll you have, gents?" she inquired of Jake and Gomez.

"Just a cup of nearcaf, *chiquita*," the curly-haired detective responded.

"The New England tofu chowder is awfully good tonight—oops, I mean this morning," she said, laughing. "It's almost two a.m. already. And you, sir?"

Jake said, "Nearcaf for now."

"Oaky doak. My name's Patsy and if you think of anything else, just give a yell." Smiling, she went walking away from their booth.

The little restaurant was narrow and sat close to the beach in the Malibu Sector. It was less than a half-mile from the condo Jake shared with his son.

"I miss the old waitress." Gomez sighed and scratched at his moustache.

"You mean that rattletrap robot?"

"Suzanne was her name. She worked here for years and was noted for her adoration of me."

"Most waitresses, mechanical and otherwise, are fond of you."

"*Sí, es verdad,*" agreed his partner. "They junked Suzanne. She's on a scrap heap someplace."

"Everything ends up on a scrap heap eventually."

Gomez said, "Well, enough philosophizing, *amigo*.

From what you've been telling me and what I've been telling you about our quest for the truth—we don't have a
single damn useful clue as to where the hell Jill might be.''

''Right, so it's time to report her disappearance to the
SoCal cops.''

''Her husband has probably already taken care of that,
but even so—Oh, *gracias*, Pasty.''

The pretty android was setting down their mugs of nearcaf. ''Anybody like a soy-abalone sandwich to go with
this?''

''Not at this time, no,'' Jake informed her.

''To stay on the good side of the local minions of the
law,'' observed Gomez after sipping from his cup, ''we had
better make a report. Damn, I wish to hell we'd been able
to track Jill down.''

''You rescued her a lot when you were married, Sid,''
Jake reminded his partner. ''It won't hurt to let somebody
else take over this time.''

''I know, but now that we're damn sure there are some
powerful Tek people involved—hell, I'm worried that
they'll kill her or at least hurt her seriously.''

''We'll talk to Bascom at the agency in the morning,''
said Jake. ''Because of the Tek angle, he's more than likely
to let us go on working on this.''

''The possibility of turning a buck always appeals to the
jefe,'' agreed Gomez. ''I wonder if I really might want a
bowl of New—''

''Gosh, look at that, would you?'' The android waitress
was standing at the front window of the little café, pointing
out at the night sky.

Gomez left his seat, moving toward her. *''Caramba,''* he
exclaimed.

Dropping down out of the fog were three black skyvans,

spotlights sweeping the beach and the front of the AllNite Neptune, sirens bleating.

Jake joined his partner at the front of the place. "Cops," he said.

"Trouble," added Gomez.

— 6 —

SAND CAME SPRAYING up as the first of the trio of SoCal State Police skyvans set down a hundred feet from the front door of the Allnite Neptune Café.

"Golly, this is the very first police raid I've ever witnessed," said the android waitress.

"Stay inside here, *cara*, and savor it," suggested Gomez as he followed Jake out into the foggy night.

The other two police vans were landing, swinging their spotlight beams to catch the two emerging Cosmos detectives.

From the nearest skyvan came a lean black officer. "Just what in the hell are you two tricky bastards up to this time?"

"*Buenas noches*, Lieutenant Drexler." Gomez gave him a lazy salute.

Jake nodded toward the café. "I hear the New England tofu chowder is pretty good tonight."

Detective Lieutenant Drexler, fists clenched at his side, came walking right up to him. Three uniformed cops, carrying stunguns, backed him up. "You, Gomez," he said, pointing an accusing finger. "Your wife was kidnapped hours ago, but you didn't even bother to notify us."

"*Former* wife," corrected Gomez. "My current wife is safely at home."

Drexler made an angry noise. "Spare me the bullshit, Gomez," he said. "You knew that a woman had been abducted. You're supposed to report that sort of—"

"No, all I knew for sure was that her vidphone call to me was interrupted," he cut in. "I decided to see if I could find out what had happened before I brought in the law. Less embarrassing that way, in case—"

"Yeah, I remember Jill Bernardino," said Drexler. "She used to be a Tekhead and she got in all sorts of trouble."

"That's true, *sí*."

The police lieutenant frowned at Jake. "There's a good chance this whole business tonight is tied in with Tek," he suggested. "What do you know about it, Cardigan?"

"Not as much as I'd like."

"Jake is just along to lend me a hand," explained Gomez. "This isn't official Cosmos business."

"Probably because that boss of yours, Walt Bascom, can't figure out how to screw a fat fee out of anybody."

Jake looked up at the misty night sky. "Who tipped you as to our activities?"

"Her husband, right after Gomez harassed him," answered the policeman. "At least Reinman had the sense to bring us in."

"And how'd you know we were at this joint?" inquired Gomez.

"Went to Cardigan's place first," replied Drexler. "That kid of yours, Cardigan, is nearly as stubborn as you when it comes to—"

"If you hurt him, Drexler . . ." Jake started to lunge for the cop.

Gomez caught him by the arm, held him back. "*Cuidado*, Jake," he advised. "I'm sure the lieutenant knows better than to try anything rough with Dan."

"I never touched him," said Drexler. "But, since he's enrolled at the SoCal Police Academy, it might be a good idea if he practiced being a little more respectful to real police officers."

"We'll pass that cogent advice along," promised Gomez. "Now, *por favor*, what do you know about the whereabouts of Jill Bernardino?"

"Not a hell of a lot," admitted the lieutenant. "If you'd brought us in as soon as you knew she'd been taken, we'd be a lot closer to finding her by now. I've got a forensic crew out there going over that half-assed park."

Jake gestured at the police vans. "Maybe you ought to put some of these lads to work on the thing."

Ignoring him, Drexler asked Gomez, "What did she say to you when she called for help?"

"Hardly anything," he answered with a shrug. "Only that she thought she was being followed."

"By who—Tek people?"

"She didn't have time to supply any details."

Drexler took a step closer to Gomez. "And why in the hell was she there at all?"

"Jill's back writing for the vidwall, Lieutenant. I'm pretty sure she was expecting to meet somebody with background information for a script she was working on."

"The Hollywood Starwalk Park isn't exactly a research center," said Lieutenant Drexler. "C'mon, Gomez, what was she doing there?"

"I don't know," Gomez told him. "This was the first time I've even so much as spoken to her in years. If you want information on her recent activities, talk to her husband."

"She never struck me as the type who'd confide much in her husband," said the policeman with a short, dry laugh. "Or wasn't that your impression when you were married to the lady?"

Jake said, "Our nearcaf is getting cold, Drexler. Shouldn't you fellows be out looking for clues?"

Making another angry sound, the cop turned away and started for his skyvan. He stopped, turned. "I'm mad now," he told them slowly and evenly. "But if you guys keep holding out on me—I'm going to shift into being truly pissed off. Then you'd better watch out."

Jake grinned. "Thanks for the warning," he said, and went back inside the café.

They were settling into their booth and Gomez was reaching for his nearcaf mug, when Jake's pocket phone buzzed.

"Yeah?"

Bascom's scowling face appeared on the tiny screen. "Is Gomez with you?"

"Yeah."

"I want to see you two buffoons in my office."

"We'll be dropping in first thing in the morning, Chief," Jake assured him.

"You'll be dropping in within the next half hour," corrected the head of the Cosmos Detective Agency. "If not sooner."

— 7 —

DAWN WAS MOVING slowly into Greater Los Angeles and the fog was gradually thinning away. Walt Bascom was standing gazing out of one of the high, wide windows when Gomez and Jake entered his office in Tower II of the Cosmos Detective Agency Building. He had his hands clasped behind his back.

"What does he remind you of?" Gomez asked his partner, settling into a chair facing the agency chief's large metal desk.

"One of those heroic statues they used to put up in public parks in centuries gone by?" Jake straddled a chair.

"No, it's more like a wooden figurehead on an ancient ship that—"

"When you two clowns end your detecting careers— which could be any day now," said Bascom, turning to glower at them, "you can work up this sort of witty patter into an act for the vidwall."

Jake grinned. "You know, Sid, for a while there I was starting to think he was mellowing."

"*Sí*, so did I. But this is the old gruff martinet we've come to love and cherish."

Bascom, slowly and precisely, came walking back to his desk. He was a tan, wrinkled man in his fifties and at the moment, his deep scowl added substantial new wrinkles to the large collection he already had. "Tell me, lads, are you intending to go into the private gumshoe business on your own?"

"Our loyalty is to Cosmos," Jake assured him.

Gomez said, "I've been thinking of having *Cosmos Forever* tattooed on my—"

"Well, if you're still working for *me*," said the chief, voice rising, "then why in the holy hell didn't you let me know the minute you found out Jill Bernardino had been kidnapped?"

"It started out as a sort of personal thing, *jefe*. Jill's an ex-wife of mine and—"

"I know who she is, for Christ sake, Sid," said Bascom. "Didn't I help you bail her out of the pokey at least half a dozen times during your days of wedded bliss?"

"Sure, but still I—"

"More importantly," continued the agency boss, "there is a Tek angle to all this." He leaned forward, resting his palms flat out on the desktop. "I've got a hunch your one-time mate's disappearance may just connect with some of the interesting rumors that have been finding their way to me in recent days."

"*Qué pasa?*" Gomez straightened up in his chair, watching Bascom.

"Nobody has many details as yet, but it seems that certain potent European Tek cartels have something large and unsavory in the works."

"Yeah, that fits in with what we've been picking up tonight," Jake told him. "The odds are that one or more

European Tek outfits are involved in whatever's happened to Jill.''

"And we've also been hearing about some large-scale Tek venture starting up overseas," added Gomez.

Bascom seated himself, steepling his fingers. "It's likely that Jill stumbled on some facts about this latest Tek shenanigan while doing her research on the Sonny Hokori documovie."

"You already know about the Hokori project, huh?" said Jake.

"When will you toddlers accept the fact that I'm infallible and omniscient?"

"Okay, so tell us where Jill is," requested Gomez.

"Well, maybe not a hundred percent omniscient just yet," conceded the Cosmos chief. "But inching ever closer."

"Why exactly," asked Jake, "are you taking such an interest in this particular mess?"

"I could say because I used to know poor Jill and I'm concerned for her welfare," answered Bascom. "But that's only part of it. However, when I found out what you fellas were poking into, it struck me that the agency ought to be able to parlay this into at least one substantial fee."

"We were thinking along those same lines," said Gomez. "You have connections with several sneaky and sly government intelligence agencies—the kind that the President and his spokespeople are always denying exist. They'd pay for information on a new and unsuspected Tek plot."

"Very good, Sid," said Bascom. "Apparently you're not quite as dumb as your behavior earlier tonight led me to believe."

Jake eyed him. "You've already set up a deal with somebody back in DC, haven't you, Walt?"

"Hey, *amigo*," complained his partner. "Before you *hombres* start toting up how much we're going to make on this caper—how about defending me against this slur on my IQ?"

Jake grinned and ignored him. "Well, Walt?"

"Yep, I've been in contact with a chap in Washington. He runs a very secret and powerful intelligence agency." He rubbed his hands together, producing a dry, rasping sound. "They're going to pay us a really impressively large fee. If, that is, we provide them with some solid stuff before they can dig it up themselves."

"*Muy bien,*" observed Gomez. "But suppose it turns out that Jill was actually just carried off by a jilted boyfriend?"

"Well, in that event we'll still collect a hefty sum from Ernst Reinman. I contacted him a couple hours ago and persuaded him that Cosmos could find his missing wife long before the police," Bascom informed them. "It's possible Reinman is dipping into the Starvation Center coffers, by the way, since he sure didn't balk at the hefty price I quoted him."

"You mean," asked Gomez, frowning, "we'll also be working for Jill's present husband?"

Bascom said, "Exactly, and I had to do a terrific selling job to convince him you were qualified to work on this one, Sid. He doesn't think much of you—either as a sleuth or a human being."

"*Ai,* my former *esposa* told him considerable falsehoods about me." He sighed. "You would think, though, that once he encountered me in the flesh and face to face, he'd have sensed my saintly aura."

Yawning once, Jake rose up. "We've got some further leads to follow up on," he said. "I think, however, that I'd like to grab a few hours' sleep before continuing."

"Sleep as long as you like," said Bascom. "Just so you

report back here by tomorrow afternoon with a hell of a lot more information than you've come up with so far.''

The faceless man said, "It would be a real good idea, Cardigan, to forget all about Jill Bernardino."

Jake sat up in bed, grabbing his stungun off the night table.

The man, whose head was a blur of pink and orange dots, had appeared unbidden on the vidphone across the early-morning room. "Nobody wants to die," he added in a rumbling doctored voice. "Think about it, asshole."

"Who you working for?" asked Jake.

The screen went black.

Leaving his bed, Jake moved to the phone. Resting the gun on his bare knee, he punched out a number on the keyboard.

Seconds later a smiling copper-plated robot showed up on the screen. "Cosmos Detective Agency/Security Department," it said. "Top of the morning to you, Mr. Cardigan."

"Some goon just made an intruder call to my number two home number," he said. "Find out how they managed that—and who."

"Coming right up. Will you wait?"

"Nope, call me again in fifteen minutes."

Jake shed the pajama top he slept in, took a quick lite-shower and dressed. He slipped the stungun into his shoulder holster.

When he stepped out onto the deck of the condo, his son was sitting there drinking a plazcup of citrisub.

"A person your age, Dad, really needs more than two hours of sleep." Dan, a lean young man of sixteen, was wearing his SoCal Police Academy uniform.

"I got an unexpected wake-up call." Walking to the rail, he scanned the surrounding beach.

"What's wrong?"

"Oh, just some lout trying to dissuade me."

"You on a new case?"

Nodding, Jake told him about the disappearance of Jill Bernardino and what he and Gomez had accomplished thus far in trying to find out what had become of her.

"One of Gomez' wives, huh? Did I ever meet her?"

"Years ago, yeah."

"She's the redhead, right?"

"No, that was Georgine, Gomez' third wife."

Dan shook his head. "Then I don't think I remember her."

The deck phone buzzed.

"Yeah?" answered Jake.

The Cosmos bot smiled. "The phone call in question was made from a landvan in the Long Beach Sector of Greater Los Angeles," it reported. "The vehicle was found abandoned a few moments ago. Listed as stolen from the Altadena Sector late last evening."

"And how'd they break through my screening system?"

"What was used, Mr. Cardigan, was one of these new gate-crasher phones."

"I'm supposed to be resistant to gadgets like that."

"So we thought, too," replied the bot. "Your entire security system is being reevaluated from here. We'll get all the kinks out of it, never fear."

"Great, that gives me enormous peace of mind." He hung up.

"Some of the Teklords are unhappy with you again," observed his son.

"I'm on the permanent shit list of a lot of the cartels." Jake looked out toward the brightening Pacific. "But this particular warning was prompted by our hunting for Jill.''

''It's possible, isn't it, that Gomez' ex-wife is doing something illegal herself? From what you've told me about her Tek habit and all.''

''Supposedly Jill is no longer hooked on the stuff,'' he said to his son. ''She's clean, upright and gainfully employed.''

''Sure, but she's not faithful to the guy she's married to now,'' Dan pointed out. ''That means, to me anyway, that she can't be trusted.''

Jake grinned a thin grin. ''I sure as hell wouldn't trust her, no.''

Dan stood up. ''How are you and Bev Kendricks getting along?''

''We have ceased to be a romantic twosome, I'm afraid.''

''That's too bad. She's a terrific person—and you can trust her.''

''That you can,'' his father agreed. ''The problem is that she thinks I'm still moping too much over Beth Kittridge's death.''

''Well, you are, you know.''

''I am, yeah,'' he agreed. ''I'm probably going to have to talk to somebody—somebody professional—about it.''

''When?''

''Right after,'' he promised, ''we clear up this case.''

— 8 —

THERE WAS NOTHING but darkness.

She awakened to it.

The blackness was warm and impenetrable and Jill Bernardino was sprawled in the center of it. Very tentatively, she felt around her.

She seemed to be lying facedown on a smooth surface, probably a metal floor.

Her head ached, but she was feeling much more pain than that. Her hands, arms, legs, were pulsing with pain and her ribs hurt. Breathing, now that she was aware of doing it again, was painful, too. Her lungs didn't feel as though they were working properly anymore.

"Stungun," she murmured.

They'd used a stungun on her last night.

Was it last night, though?

She realized she had no clear idea of how long she'd been unconscious. No notion of how long she'd been here.

Wherever here was.

There'd been two of them who'd caught up with her at that run-down park. One was a big, hulking robot—dented, painted a milky green—who walked with a lurching, wobbly gait. The other was a short, ugly man, bald with a smear of whiskers on his chinless face. He was the one who'd shot her.

"Want to try to run for it, love?" he'd asked, chuckling, pointing the big silvery stungun at her from across the room.

Jill hadn't moved, but he'd used the gun anyway.

She shuddered now, remembering the brief, intense wave of pain she'd felt as the beam from the silvery gun touched her just below her left breast.

Jill pushed at the floor with her palms, struggling against the aches that produced. She managed, eventually, to sit up.

The surrounding blackness was as thick as ever. She could see absolutely nothing.

Leaning forward, she began, very slowly, to crawl on her hands and knees. She didn't think she was ready to stand up and walk just yet.

After crawling about ten feet, pausing frequently to feel at the darkness in front of her, she came in contact with a wall.

A smooth metal wall that felt very much like the floor.

Breathing through her mouth, still experiencing considerable pain in her chest, she turned and sat with her back to the wall.

She, for some reason, remembered Gomez then.

Yes, she'd called him just before they'd run her to ground.

Jill and Gomez hadn't had an especially happy or calm marriage, but she'd liked him. Trusted him, too, which is more than he'd have been able to say of her. He'd helped her out of a lot of bad situations.

"Terrible situations," she said softly. "And too damned many of them."

She still had faith in him. If anybody could find her, find her and get her free of this, it would be Gomez.

Her husband was all right, but she knew he'd never be able to handle anything like rescuing her. That was why she'd turned to Gomez.

Jill decided to attempt standing.

She was only halfway to her feet when a door suddenly slid swiftly open and a large glaring rectangle of harsh yellow light blossomed in the opposite wall.

The village of Ralfminster was in the Somerset district of England. And the quaint thatched cottage, surrounded by a picturesque low stone wall, sat on the outskirts with nothing but rolling hills and hedgerows stretching away all around it.

Early on that clear spring afternoon a heavyset man, wearing a thick coat sweater, came shuffling out of the back door of the cottage. He was in his middle seventies somewhere and the tufts of hair that showed beneath his checkered cap were white.

Following close behind him came a younger man. He was carrying a folding chair, a folded metal easel, a partially done canvas, a realwood box of paints and brushes and a palm-size black control box. "Same spot as usual, Mr. Anzelmo?"

"What do you think, peckerhead?" Anzelmo halted on a patch of green lawn.

There was a large blond man sitting on the fence a hundred or so feet away. He had a stunrifle resting in his lap.

"Hey, Toby," called Anzelmo, "am I paying you to sit around on your fat ass?"

"No, Mr. Anzelmo. Sorry, sir." Toby hopped free of the wall and started pacing along it.

The man carrying all the painting gear had opened the

chair and placed it on the lawn. He was now concentrating on arranging the easel.

"The chair belongs two feet to the frigging right, Julie." The older man was gazing out at the fields and the stand of oak trees just beyond the wall.

"Right you are, sir." Julie moved the chair. "That about it?"

"What do you think, shitcan?"

After studying the chair, Julie bent and nudged it an inch and a half to the left. "Looks about perfect now."

"Nothing you had a hand in could come anywhere near to being perfect." Anzelmo lowered himself into the seat. "But it'll do."

Nodding, the younger man put the canvas in place. "There we are," he said while setting the box of painting materials on a small shelf attached to the left arm of the chair.

Anzelmo was scowling, looking from his painting to the oak trees. "Julie, how many trees do you see in my painting?"

He hunched, squinting at the picture. "Six, Mr. Anzelmo."

"Okay, and how many are there by the wall?"

After a quick count, Julie answered, "Five, sir."

"What can we do about that, jerk-off?"

The younger man grabbed up the control box from where he'd left it on the grass. He touched at the keys.

Three new holographic oaks sprouted next to the others.

"Oops. Too many. Sorry." His fingers touched the keys again and two trees vanished. "There."

"I'm thinking maybe seven would be better," reflected Anzelmo. "Put in another one and I'll add it to my picture."

"Yes, sir."

A fresh sturdy oak returned to join the rest.

Julie inquired, "Anything else?"

The older man was eyeing the nearest meadow. "I'm pretty darn good at painting sheep."

"You're very good. We've all commented on your ability to—"

"Horseshit," cut in Anzelmo. "I can just see you bunch of wankers sitting around of an evening talking about my painting. Anyhow, I want some sheep up there in the goddamn meadow."

"How many, sir?"

"You decide."

Julie swallowed once, then again. He used the control box and a flock of white holographic sheep materialized up in the sloping meadow. Some slept, some roamed, some munched at the grass.

After a moment Anzelmo said, "Count them, will you."

Julie counted. "Thirteen, sir."

"Thirteen is unlucky. Are you trying to put a jinx on me?"

The keys were worked again. "How do you feel about eleven?"

"They'll do. Now get your skinny butt back inside," ordered Anzelmo. "I'm going to paint for exactly forty-five minutes and I don't want to see you anywhere near me until then."

Julie hurried away.

"What a kiss-ass," murmured Anzelmo as he selected a brush.

Less than ten minutes later Julie came hurrying out of the thatched cottage. He was carrying a palmphone. "Mr. Anzelmo?"

The older man continued to paint, ignoring him.

Stopping next to the chair, Julie held out the phone. "This is a call you had better take, sir."

Anzelmo continued to ignore him, concentrating on rendering the wool on one of the sheep.

"It has to do with Jill Bernardino, sir."

Very slowly and carefully, Anzelmo lowered the brush and scowled up at him. "What about her?"

"Kaltenborn out in Greater LA will explain. But it looks like things have gone wrong."

Anzelmo grabbed the phone. "What in the hell are you bothering me for?"

The husky black man who was looking, uneasily, out at him from the tiny phonescreen said, "We don't have her, sir."

"Did you ever have her, shitcan?"

"No, somebody else got her."

"Who?"

"We aren't sure as yet," answered the black man. "When we moved in to take Jill Bernardino—well, it turned out someone else had gotten to her first."

Anzelmo asked him, "Who runs the biggest, most powerful Tek cartel in England?"

"You do, obviously, sir," answered both Kaltenborn and Julie.

Leaning forward in his folding chair, Anzelmo asked the phone, "Then who the hell in America—in frigging Greater Los Angeles of all places—has the balls to go up against me?"

"We're in the process of finding out. Until we—"

"You're going to be in the process of attending your own damned funeral," promised the Teklord. "Unless you locate that bitch and shut her up for good and all."

"That's what we're trying to do, sir."

"Could the SoCal cops have grabbed her—or somebody

from the International Drug Control Agency?''

"We don't think so.''

"Well, find her.'' He killed the call. "Help me up out of this chair, Julie. I'm through painting for today.''

— 9 —

BY MIDDAY THERE was a thin yellow haze covering most of Greater Los Angeles. Jake's skycar was rising up through it, climbing away from the Visitors Lot at the Venice Sector Campus of the University of California, when the voxbox announced, "Important communication from Timecheck."

"Put him through."

The lean Chinese popped up on the phonescreen. He was checking one of the watches built into his metal arm. "Geez, Jake, your response time is really drag-ass," the informant told him. "Twenty-three seconds. Not so good."

"Excuse it." Jake guided his car up to an altitude of 5,000 feet. The farther you got from the artificial canals of the Venice Sector, the less woebegone they looked. "I was on the verge of getting in touch with you myself."

"Let me pass on my bulletin first," requested Timecheck. "I'm a little reluctant, since you may get the notion that I'm no longer a reliable source of—"

"Some of what you told me last night turns out not to be true?"

Timecheck paused to tap one of his watch faces with his forefinger. "Tokyo's quit ticking again."

"Get back to what the hell it is you're apologizing for."

"Listen, Jake, every word of what I passed along is the absolute and unvarnished truth," assured Timecheck. "However, subsequent data I've been collecting leads me to believe that I probably, through no fault of my own, nudged you along a wrong path."

Jake grinned in a bleak way. "Explain."

"Okay, it is still God's own truth that a pack of Europe-based Teklords sent out orders to pick up this Jill Bernardino lady," continued the informant. "The thing is, Jake—well, sir, somebody beat them to it."

"Who exactly?"

"I'm at work on that aspect," said Timecheck. "So far it looks like a local cartel got to her first."

"A SoCal Tek outfit?"

"Almost certainly, yes."

"Thanks for filling me in." Jake nodded thoughtfully. "Anything more on what these European Teklords are really up to—or why they were planning to abduct Jill?"

"Not yet, but they're cooking up something mammoth," answered Timecheck. "So, what are you following up at the moment?"

"Trying to locate Jeffrey Monkwood," he told the phonescreen. "But Jill's professorial beau didn't show up to teach his Advanced Communications class today. Nor did he bother to notify the university that he wasn't going to drop in. Nobody has any idea where the hell he might be."

"You try his house in the Glendale Sector?"

"I phoned and got no response. I'm heading there now to look around."

"I've dug up a few more facts about the prof," volunteered Timecheck. "The one that'll do you the most good right now is that he and his wife no longer reside under the same roof. She has a place down in the Palm Springs Sector.''

''If I don't find out anything at his setup, I'll try her.''

''And, Jake,'' cautioned the Chinese, ''now that we're getting even more Tek people coming abroad—be extra careful, huh?''

The home medibot was a cheap reconditioned model, all she could afford just now. It stood an inch or so under three feet in height and its white enameled surface had a yellowish tinge. ''I'm coming, I'm coming,'' the bot was saying in a fuzzy, rattling voice. ''I'm not as spry as I used to be.''

''Hurry . . . please,'' gasped Eleanor Monkwood. ''Starting . . . to have . . . breathing trouble again.'' She was a blonde woman in her early thirties, thin and pale, standing now in the doorway that led to the tiny sundeck of the three-room domed house.

''If you'd stay in here where the aircirc system provides breathable air,'' the medibot told her as it waddled nearer, ''you wouldn't have these respiratory problems, lady.''

''Wanted . . . some sun.''

''Smog's all you get when you stray outside on a day like this.'' When the little white robot reached her, it poked at a button in its side. ''Darn, this thing's stuck again.''

Eleanor held on tight to the doorframe with both thin hands. She could barely inhale at all now and she was growing dizzy. ''Hurry . . .''

''I'm not a top-of-the-line mech,'' the bot reminded, whapping itself in the side a few times with one metal fist. ''There, that's popped her.'' A panel swung open and the bot reached in to pull out an oxikit. ''Here you go, lady.''

She hesitated, then carefully and slowly let go with one

hand, bent and reached out to grasp the breathing mask/oxygen container unit. "Can you . . . help me . . . put it on?"

"You're going to have to tilt over a bit more." The medibot's stubby arms didn't reach to her face, even though it was now standing on tiptoe.

Eleanor leaned, then started swaying. She suddenly started to topple forward.

The bot hopped aside, let her fall.

She hit flat out and facedown on the grey carpeting. Her mouth was open and she was trying to breathe in air.

"You're really a mess today, lady." The bot squatted, picked up the oxikit. It rolled her over on her back, attached the mask and clicked on the oxygen.

Slowly, painfully, Eleanor's breathing improved. The dizziness passed and she sat up. "Thanks . . ."

"Now let's see if you can stand all the way up. That's it, hold on to me."

Pressing her hand down on the metal shoulder of the mechanical man, she managed to push herself upright.

"Okay, we'll take a stroll over to your chair." It managed to guide her across the living room to a metal chair that faced the viewindow.

From there you got a view of dozens of other small dome houses, patches of dry yellow desert and a good deal of cactus. There were also several holographic Joshua trees out there.

Leaving her in the chair, the robot wobbled over to shut the door to the deck. "There'll be a heck of a lot less trouble for the both of us, lady, if you'd follow the Medplan you were given."

"I'm sorry. . . . It's just that I never had smog-asthma until I moved out here three months ago," she said in a weary voice. "Takes some getting . . . used to."

"Here we go again," remarked the medibot, turning its back on the view. "Self-pity time in the desert. Going to blame your husband for dumping you and giving you such a trauma that you acquired this malady."

"Jeffrey didn't dump me," she corrected. "I left him."

The little robot shook its ball of a head. "You're not living in the right century, lady," it observed. "Why let a little harmless adultery bother you? Instead you should've used it to get more of what you want out of life. 'You're rolling in the hay with assorted bimbos, Jeff—so now I want a bigger house, a skycar of my own and all the stuff on this list!' That's the way to handle things."

Eleanor didn't reply.

After a moment the bot remarked, "If you can keep from having any more fits for an hour or so, I'll get back to tidying up your sloppy bedroom."

She said, breathing mask muffling her voice, "I'm fine."

"You sure don't look it." The medibot took three steps toward the bedroom door and then ceased to function.

The aircirc system died at the same instant.

"What's wrong?" Eleanor started to stand up.

The door to the deck came slapping open. A large, wide robot, painted a pale green, came lumbering into the room. "Sit down," he boomed.

Behind him came a small bald man with a frizzy moustache and a trace of a beard. "Afternoon, love," he said, smiling and holding up his silvery stungun. "We thought we'd drop in for a bit of a chat, don't you know."

═10═

GOMEZ HESITATED ON the threshold of the toyshop, frowning down at the fuzzy little mechanical puppy. "Hey, *perrito*, what are you doing to my boot?"

"Using it to teethe on, schlep," replied the toy dog in a deep roughhouse voice.

"Your voxbox needs some urgent fine tuning." With a terse kicking motion, the detective managed to send the pup sailing across the Wondersmith's Toyshop showroom.

"Cheezit!" cried a two-foot-high Fairy Princess who was occupying a little gilt throne atop a slowly rotating plaz pedestal. "It's some kind of perverted molester come to abuse us one and all."

"Keep your knickers on, sis," advised an overstuffed red-headed rag doll who was slumped in a slowly ticking little tin rocker. "I know this dorf. He's an old patron."

"He looks like an *ancient* patron to me." The puppy was huddled behind a toy white piano, glowering at Gomez. "He's got more wrinkles than a relief map of a senile prune."

"*Niños y niñas*, it truly warms my heart to exchange all

these pleasantries with yous,'' the detective assured them. ''But I actually dropped by in response to a summons from your boss.''

''Nertz,'' said the princess.

''Don't let these little hooligans razz you, honey.'' A large, fat woman with a good deal of crinkly silver hair emerged from the toyshop office, arms spread wide and smiling at him. Her three-piece sinsilk suit was a mixture of bright citrus hues. ''G'wan, you imps, back to your posts. Look cuddly and desirable for our customers.''

''Corky, we haven't had any customers since those half-wits this morning,'' reminded the rag doll. ''Couple of aging dimbulbs from the San Berdoo Sector who decided I was too flamboyant for their pansy grandson.''

Corky Keepnews bent to give his chair a slap that set it to rocking at a more rapid rate. ''You can't refer to prospective customers as 'a pair of old farts' and expect them to ask me to gift wrap you, kiddo. Let's hole up in my office, Gomez, I want to talk to you.''

Her toyshop was up on the seventeenth level of the Westwood Sector Mall. From the one narrow viewindow you could see part of the University of SoCal Campus #26, where either a riot or a rally was in progress in the glade.

As soon as Corky had settled in behind her new pink neowood desk, Gomez asked, ''Why the urgent need to see me, *calabaza*?'' He settled into a tin rocker, a grown-up version of the one the rag doll occupied out in the showroom.

''We've been buddies and business associates for a heck of a long time, darling,'' the fat woman told him.

''You're just about my most reliable informant.''

Corky's chair made small groaning noises as she shifted her weight and rested a plump elbow on the desktop. ''I just came across some information that pertains to you and that reckless partner of yours,'' she said, lowering her voice some. ''It has to do with this case you're working on.''

His left eye narrowed. ''What case would that be, *cara*?''

''Hey, you don't have to be cute with me, honey. I know you're trying to find that hot-pants bitch that you used to—''

''What do you know about Jill's kidnapping?'' He left the rocker, moved closer to her desk.

''The most important thing I know,'' Corky said, ''is that some people are going to do their damnedest to throw a spanner in your works. They want you to quit—and if they have to they'll do you some serious harm.''

''How serious?''

''You might end up graveyard-dead, dear.''

Perching on the edge of the pink desk, he leaned toward her and studied her plump face with narrowed eyes. ''Who are these *pendejos*?''

Corky's voice dropped even lower. ''You're messing with a big Tek cartel here.''

''I already know that—a combo of European outfits who seem to—''

''Nope, that's not what you have to worry about, Gomez,'' she assured him. Then held up a hand in a wait-a-minute gesture. ''Well, let's amend that. Sure, you've got to worry about them, because they want to get their hands on your ex, too. But there's danger much nearer to home.''

''Somebody else got to her first, somebody local?''

Corky nodded, her chair jiggling. ''Way I hear it, honey, it's that runt who calls himself Johnny Trocadero.''

''*Sí*, the little *hombre* who runs the San Diego Sector Tek cartel,'' said Gomez, frowning. ''So what do we have here, Cork, Teklords going up against each other?''

''All I know is that dear little Jill must know something that several nasty bastards are anxious to find out about.''

"Trocadero grabbed her?"

"He hired the goons who did the job."

"And they are?"

She glanced toward the closed door of her office. "I think it was a weasel named Dunkirk. He usually works with a rumdum robot that he built himself."

"Skinny *pendejo* who doesn't even know how to grow a decent moustache?" Gomez fingered his own moustache.

"That's him, hon," she answered. "And before you bother to ask—no, I don't know where they took her."

"This Dunkirk—is he also the one who's planning to do me and Jake harm?"

"That's what I've picked up, kid."

"Anything else you've come across that I ought to know?"

Corky said, "You better watch out for a lady called Yedra Cortez. Very nasty critter from your homeland who is the brains *and* the muscle of Trocadero's whole setup."

"I've seen that *puta* before," Gomez said, standing up. "How much do I owe you for this wealth of information, Corky? It's enough to make a paranoid of any man and ought to be worth a tidy fee."

"So far it's on the house, lover. For old time's sake and as a little gift to a damned good customer." She stood, too. "If you want any more—it's going to be a thousand dollars."

"Top price, huh?"

"It wouldn't take much for any and all of these lowlifes to put my name on their shit lists right next to yours, Gomez," she explained as she came around her desk and took hold of his arm. "If I'm going to get killed, I ought to make as much as I can off it."

"Sound business philosophy." He allowed her to escort him out of the toyshop.

• • •

The small bald man smiled sweetly as he tightened his grip on Eleanor Monkwood's upper arm. "That's a terribly bad wheeze you got there, love."

The big green robot was looming on the other side of her chair. "It's the bloomin' air in these parts," he rumbled, tapping his broad metal chest with a fist. "Affects my breathing setup something awful at times."

The thin woman said, "What . . . do you . . . want?"

"Now, dear, you'll have me believing that you're not paying close enough attention."

"We already told you," reminded the big bot, "what we want."

"That's absolutely true," seconded the bald, sparsely whiskered man. "I informed you soon as we arrived that we'd popped in for a bit of conversation."

Eleanor said nothing, concentrating on letting the oxikit help her to breathe.

"To continue." He increased the pressure on her thin arm. "What we came to talk about is this—where's your damned husband?"

"I don't know," she answered. "Probably . . . the university."

"Naw, not so," the robot informed her, tilting toward her some.

"He's not on campus where he's supposed to be. Nobody at the school knows where he's gotten to or what's become of him."

She took a few slow, shallow breaths. "If you know . . . where my husband works . . . and you know where I live," she said, "then you . . . must know . . . that we're separated."

The bald man cocked his head to the right, frowning. "I don't know about you, mate," he said to the green robot, ''but I'm having the devil's own time understanding what this dear lady is saying.''

''Me too.''

''Why do you suppose that is?''

The bot's arm creaked when he raised his hand. ''Must be that breathing mask she's wearing.''

''I do believe you're right.'' His stroked his wispy whiskers with his fingertips. ''The bloody thing filters out most of her words, it does.''

''Shall I,'' offered the robot, raising his big metal hand again, ''rip it off?''

''No, that's all right. I can handle the job.''

Eleanor pleaded, ''No, please . . . I really won't be able to breathe without . . . it.''

The robot shook his head sympathetically. ''That's a pity for sure, mum.''

''Maybe then you'd best speak up now. Tell us what we came to find out.''

''I don't . . . know where . . . he is.''

The bald man glanced at his companion. ''Did you catch any of what she just said?''

''Nary a word, no.''

''Sorry, love.'' The bald man shook his head, sadly, and reached for the breathing mask.

But he never managed to touch it.

Instead both of his hands went flapping up above his head, his body stiffened, he gave a choking sigh, and went dropping forward.

When he fell across Eleanor's lap, she drew both knees aside and that deflected him.

He hit the side of her chair with his thinly bewhiskered chin, bounced, slammed into the floor on elbows and knees, stretched straight out and was completely and totally unconscious.

"Don't touch it," said Jake to the big green robot.

Jake was standing in the now open bedroom doorway, his stungun aimed at the mechanical man.

The robot had been in the process of opening a panel in his side and tugging out a lazgun. "You ought not to have stunned him," he said.

"I know, but every time I see a couple of louts mistreating someone—I get this uncontrollable impulse." He grinned. "Hell, there it is again."

This silent stungun beam struck the bot just above the opening in his torso. He started to rattle, taking two thumping steps to the left.

Jake sprinted over, gave the disabled mechanism a forceful shove with the palm of his free hand.

The robot smacked the floor, stretched out flat next to his partner.

"You don't have a very good security system here, Mrs. Monkwood," he told her. "Anybody can get in with very little effort."

"I'm . . . glad you . . . got through."

Walking around the fallen intruders, Jake lifted her out of the chair and carried her over to a low black sofa. "My name is Jake Cardigan," he said, setting her down carefully. "I'm an operative with the Cosmos Detective Agency."

"Yes, I've heard of . . . you," she said, leaning back. "Well, not . . . you specifically . . . but your agency."

"We're trying to find Jill Bernardino," he said, straddling a straight chair that faced her.

"That . . . whore."

"You know her?"

"I know she and . . . my husband are . . . sleeping together," answered Eleanor. "What's happened . . . to her?"

"Looks like she's been kidnapped," he said. "Possibly

by these very lads who dropped in on you. We'll be able to find that out.''

''Why do they . . . want Jeffrey?''

''Probably because somebody believes he knows what Jill knows.''

''And . . . what is . . . that?''

Jake shook his head. ''Not sure exactly. But it seems to be connected with something several big European Tek cartels are planning.''

''Tek,'' she said. ''That . . . makes sense.''

''Your husband has some—''

''While we were still together . . . he became involved with . . . a man named Ernest Shiboo. He . . . supposedly makes his living . . . supplying very sophisticated . . . androids to . . . very rich clients,'' she said. ''He lives . . . up in NorCal . . . someplace.''

''Ernie Shiboo,'' said Jake, nodding. ''He used to be fairly high up in the Hokori Tek cartel.''

''I suspected . . . he was supplying . . . Jeffrey with Tek chips.''

''That was their only association—customer and client?''

Eleanor concentrated on her breathing for a moment, leaning back farther on the sofa. ''There was . . . something else,'' she answered finally. ''Jeffrey teaches in the . . . communications area . . . and there was . . . a show business link . . . somewhere.''

''Shiboo was using him as a consultant on some project maybe?''

''By that time . . . Jeffrey and I weren't . . . He didn't . . . discuss much about . . . his activities with me.''

''You think Shiboo knew Jill Bernardino?''

''Yes . . . I suspect Jeffrey . . . introduced her to that terrible man.''

"If your husband is hiding out," asked Jake, "do you have any idea where he might go?"

"No, I never . . . knew about his hideaways," she said. "Women like Jill . . . Bernardino might . . . but not . . . me."

Jake stood up, sliding out his palmphone. "I'll arrange to have these goons transported elsewhere."

"By the police?"

"Eventually," he said, grinning. "First we'll ask them a few pertinent questions. I'll also have the agency send someone to watch over you for a while. Need a medic?"

She nodded at her little fallen medibot. "My robot can take care of me."

Jake eyed the fallen mechanism. "Doesn't look all that efficient."

"It isn't, but—"

"If you don't mind, I'll get a medic of our own to drop in," he suggested.

Eleanor managed a faint smile. "No, that would be . . . fine," she said. "And . . . if you find out that my husband is okay . . . well, I suppose . . . I'd like to know that."

—≡ 11 ≡—

THE PUDGY JAPANESE cried out, "Your flying is much too bumpy, Herky."

"Don't call me Herky," came the reply from the cabin of the skyvan. "And I don't have any damn control over turbulence, Ernie."

Ernest Shiboo sighed before bending to pick up the check-over rod, which the last bounce had caused him to drop. "Well, let's make sure you're shipshape, gumdrop," he said to the dormant android he was standing in front of.

There were twenty-one androids flying up from SoCal to NorCal in the big cargo compartment of the van. Each was a pretty blonde teenage girl, each was dressed in a black short-skirted maid's uniform.

Shiboo had to give every one a last-minute inspection. He was working along the second row of seven. He ran the small copper-tipped rod down from head to toe, holding it about an inch from the andy's body.

When it was hovering just below the waist, the rod's voxbox said, "Fanny."

"Oh, tapioca," murmured Shiboo, annoyed.

He lifted the short black skirt to inspect the android's backside. There was a large smudge of sky-blue paint on the left buttock.

Straightening up, the Japanese reached under the maid's lace collar and touched the activate spot. "Why didn't you mention, Ally, that you'd acquired an unsightly splotch on your toke?"

"Hey, is that my job?" asked the reanimated blonde. "You ginks are supposed to inspect us after each job and I'll tell you something, Ernie, most of your maintenance crew are either Tekheads or brainstimmers and they wouldn't have noticed if my entire butt had broken out in polka dots."

"You keep forgetting to address me as Mr. Shiboo, lollipop."

"Hooey."

"How'd that smear get there?"

"Ask your last client—that grabby Mr. Goodrich in the San Luis Obispo Sector," she replied. "He tried to get fresh with me in the nursery during that bash he and his missus threw last weekend. The bots had just finished painting the room."

Shiboo frowned. "Wonder why they'd paint a little girl's room blue?"

"Ask Goodrich."

Crouching, Shiboo lifted her skirt again and squinted at the blue buttock. "I have an excellent—an extremely excellent—reputation as a provider and leaser of the finest-grade androids and servos," he said, rising up. "In the last three years I've built this business up from—"

"Maybe you should've stuck to peddling Tek, gumdrop."

"That'll be enough of that sort of talk," he warned her. "How'd you get that sort of data into your head anyway?"

"Must be a virus."

Shiboo scowled at her. "Go into the workshop at the back of the van, Ally," he instructed. "Use a litegun to clean off that damned stain."

"I'm not supposed to mess with any maintenance."

"Listen, butterball, I have to deliver twenty-one tip-top android maids to Leon Marriner at his Mansion number five in the Tiburon Enclave in exactly seventeen minutes," he told her, putting one hand on her black-clad shoulder. "The head of the entire Marriner Media empire isn't going to accept an andy with a sky-blue backside *and* I'm not about to offer him one. Nor will I risk showing up with only twenty of you."

Ally, after smoothing her skirt, wandered off in the direction of the repair area.

The skyvan hit another air pocket and the floor bounced several times. She lurched, hit against another android maid, knocking her off her feet.

"Easy, easy," cautioned Shiboo as he hurried over to pick up the fallen andy. "We can't afford any dents at this late hour."

Shiboo fidgeted in the passenger seat. "I'm sorry I've been such a nag today, Herky."

"Don't call me Herky." The android who was piloting the skyvan was handsome, muscular-looking. His golden-blond hair was wavy and long. "My name is Hercules/30F and this has come up again and again at our weekly meetings with the techno-counselor."

"I know, forgive me," apologized the Japanese. "Whenever I'm worried—scared actually, in this case—I tend to turn cranky."

"You really have to learn to relax, Ernie," advised Hercules. "Besides, the odds are that the Bernardino bitch's disappearance had nothing at all to do with you, not a damn thing.''

Frowning, Shiboo shook his head. "No, I'm certain that Jill's being kidnapped has a whole lot to do with . . . well, with what Marriner and those overseas Tek bastards are up to.''

"I hate to pick on you," said the android, "but I did mention at the time that you were a jerk to confide anything in that Bernardino woman.''

"She was paying me a nice fat fee for information.''

"Information about the Sonny Hokori cartel," reminded Hercules. "A defunct operation that nobody gives a damn about anymore—certainly nobody who's in a position to knock you off or rough you up.''

"I suppose I wanted to impress her," admitted the Japanese. "So I threw in a little of what I'd been finding out about Marriner's latest project. Hints really, nothing more.''

"More than hints, Ernie, or you wouldn't be scared silly now.''

"You know, Herk, I've brought this up with our counselor quite a few times lately," Shiboo said to the android. "But you really aren't at all sympathetic to me at times.''

"Whose fault is it if I lack empathy? Did I design and build myself?''

"All right, I planned you and oversaw your construction," he acknowledged. "Still, as I recall, I built in a lot more kindness and understanding.''

"What you're trying to do now is mix our domestic problems up with our business ventures. Not smart.''

"I am, you're absolutely right.''

"All we have to worry about today is delivering these nubile maids to Marriner's number five digs," said Hercules. "We turn them over to that bossy private sec of his, collect our handsome fee and take off for Greater LA and home."

"Thelma's okay," said Shiboo. "She's been extremely helpful to us in building the business up these past couple years."

The android said, "We provide a first-rate product. We're doing Marriner and all the rest of our snooty customers a favor—it's not the other way around, Ernie."

"You're right again."

"Now quit looking like you've just come back from your own funeral," Hercules suggested. "We're going to be setting down at number five in a couple more minutes." He tapped out a landing pattern on the dash.

"Quite probably Marriner himself won't even show up at this particular mansion of his until the day of the party." Shiboo sat up straighter in his seat. "And even when he is in residence, I rarely see him."

"Besides which, nobody in the entire Marriner Media empire has any notion that you've been blabbing their secrets to Jill Bernardino."

The mansion and grounds in the Tiburon Enclave covered five and a half acres at the edge of the expanded San Francisco Bay. The home itself was an exact replica of a late-nineteenth-century Victorian mansion, and the surrounding acres included a large formal garden, a nine-hole golf course, a swimming pavilion and a woods containing quite a few tall simulated redwoods.

The visitors' landing area was surrounded by holographic cypress trees.

After going through the recognition and permission routines, Hercules brought the skyvan in for a landing.

The landing wasn't especially smooth and two of the android maids back in the cargo area went crashing to the floor with considerable thunking and rattling.

"Herky, you've really got to improve your landing techniques." Shiboo unhooked from the safety gear and ran into the other room to get the fallen andies to their feet and check for damage.

Then he came back into the cabin and released the door on his side.

It opened to reveal the short, stocky Thelma Glanzman standing out in the sunny afternoon. Hands on hips, looking up at him. "Hello, Ernest," she said.

"Thelma, gumdrop, how are you?" said Shiboo, climbing out of the skyvan. "Just wait until you get a look at this batch of—"

"Get up to the house right away quick," she told him. "Marriner wants to talk to you."

— ☰ 12 ☰ —

AN IMAGE OF the bald, scraggly-whiskered man, half life size, appeared on one of the holograph stages in Bascom's tower office.

Circling the round stage, the Cosmos Detective Agency chief said, "This comely lad's name is Nigel Dunkirk. He—"

"Bingo," said Gomez from the chair where he was slouching.

Bascom eyed him. "What are you trying to convey?"

"You've just confirmed—which I was already near certain of anyway—that he's the *mierda* that Corky warned me about."

Jake was straddling a chair a few feet farther back from the stage. "This Dunkirk's a hired-hand type," he remarked. "Not affiliated with any particular Tek outfit."

"This time he and his *botito* are working for Johnny Trocadero."

Bascom frowned. "Why are you only now mentioning this, Sid?"

"Hey, *jefe*, I came rushing in here a few minutes ago,

bursting with news,'' the curly-haired detective reminded
his boss. ''But I was informed that Jake had dragged in this
pendejo and his faithful mechanical companion and that
you were going to brief us before we got down to—''

''Okay, enough.'' Bascom consulted his handful of print-
out memos. ''Dunkirk and the bot are reposing down in
Interrogation Suite 3 at the moment. Soon as our medics
bring the guy out of his stungun swoon, we'll troop down
there and ask him some pertinent questions.''

''He knows where Jill is,'' said Gomez.

''He at least knows where they delivered her,'' observed
Jake. ''What's the robot's name?''

Bascom's frown deepened. ''What the hell has that got
to do with anything?''

''I'm curious.''

The chief riffled the memos. ''Turns out the damn thing
doesn't have a name. Satisfied?''

''You can tell a lot about people from what they name
things.'' Jake grinned.

''We're already scanning the bot's brain to see what he
knows.''

''Timecheck told me there was a SoCal Teklord involved
in this,'' he told his partner. ''Johnny Trocadero must be
the one.''

''*Sí*, but I'm still not clear as to why he's risking going
up against the overseas Tek *hombres*.''

Bascom said, ''My prospective DC customer will want
to know about that. So find out, fellas.''

''First,'' put in Gomez, ''we have to talk to this Dunkirk
cabrón and find out where Jill is.''

The vidphone on Bascom's desk suddenly started talking. ''Lieutenant Drexler of the SoCal State Police is out
here in the reception area, Mr. Bascom. He has five officers

with him and a warrant. He says he's going to see you at once.''

There were exactly forty-two vidscreens built into the walls of the mansion's main ballroom. Each one was displaying a different Marriner Media vidshow.

Sitting in the large room's only chair, thin fingers steepled beneath his chin, was a lanky black man in a grey suit. He was a year away from thirty, his hair was close-cropped. Two men and an android stood just to the rear of his high-back wicker chair. "Screen 8," he said in his whispery voice.

The heavyset bearded man at the right of the standing trio said, "That's our *Moon Cops* show, Mr. Marriner."

Marriner's lips puckered as though he were tasting something extremely sour. "Kill it."

The thin blond man said, "But we guaranteed Selkirk at least a year of—"

"It's dead."

"I agree with you on that one," said the pink-cheeked andy. "*Moon Cops* is a dismal show, sir."

"Sure you agree with me, putz," the black man said. "That's how you were constructed."

"No, I assure you, this is an honest opinion of my own."

Marriner gave a quick whisper of a chuckle. "Screen 27," he said.

The thin blond man said, "That's *Underwater Fiesta*. This episode was filmed off the coast of—"

"Reshoot the damn thing."

The heavyset bearded man suggested, "It would be much more economical if we had the people in Enhancement punch up the existing—"

"Reshoot it."

"Yes, sir," said the thin blond man.

''Exactly what I was about to suggest,'' said the android. The room's door whirred quietly open. Thelma Glanzman appeared. ''He's here.''

''Keep him out there for a while, Thel,'' instructed Marriner. ''Screen 19.''

The secondary ballroom was not quite as large as the main one. There were only thirty vidscreens in the walls and they displayed not Marriner Media shows but variable views of what was going on inside the major Marriner offices and facilities around the world.

Marriner had a small realwood desk in the center of this ballroom and he was sitting behind it, hunched forward. Spread out atop the desk was the front page of the top-selling e-newspaper in America. ''What do you think of the headline, Ernie?''

Shiboo ran his tongue over his lips. ''Very colorful, sir.'' The Japanese was standing to the right of the desk. There were no other chairs in the big room.

''Not the typography, putz, the content.''

Shiboo cleared his throat, craned his head. '' 'Thousands Die in Tunnel Tragedy.' Very catchy, sir.''

''No, hell, it's nowhere near specific enough,'' countered the media tycoon. ''Thousands of what—people, kangaroos, nasturtiums? If it's human beings—what kind? Where?''

''Putting it that way, Mr. Marriner, the line is a bit lacking in detail, yes.''

Marriner picked up a palmphone. ''Bockman, we want a new head for the *Times-Post*. Specifics on that tunnel thing.''

Shiboo coughed into his hand.

Marriner glanced up at him. ''How many maid andies did you deliver for my upcoming bash, Ernie?''

"Twenty-one, sir."

"I understand one of them has blue spots on her ass."

"No, that's been taken care of . . . How did you know that?"

"Ernie, there isn't one damn thing about you that I don't know or can't find out," Marriner informed him. "I even know what goes on in the hay between you and that mechanized lummox of yours. Herky. Jesus."

"My relationship with him is perfectly—"

"Tell me about Jill Bernardino."

"Who?"

A whispery chuckle. "Ernie, you're not following this discussion at all as closely as you ought to be," Marriner said, pushing back a few inches in his chair. "I had hoped I'd impressed you by this time with the fact that bullshit will get you nowhere when talking to me. How much did you tell her?"

Shiboo shook his head negatively, getting the shaking all tangled up with the uncontrolled shivering that had begun. "Not a thing, Mr. Marriner," he insisted. "I mean, yes, as you seem to know, I have been providing her with information for a vidwall film she's scripting. It's about Sonny Hokori. I'm not sure if you knew him, but—"

"I knew Sonny quite well."

"Well, sir, then you know that he's dead and done for. So are most of his relatives and the top people in his Tek cartel," continued the uneasy Japanese. "Therefore, you see, I didn't think providing her with background information about the Hokori cartel would hurt anyone. Her producer was offering a very nice fee for my services and even though I only worked for Sonny in a minor capacity—"

"C'mon, Ernie, you were one of his top lieutenants. You even had a hand in framing Jake Cardigan on Tek charges and getting him sent up to the Freezer prison."

"No, no, that's not true," said Shiboo. "That was Sonny who arranged that—along with Bennett Sands and Cardigan's wife. Not me, however, sir."

"Suppose we return to Jill Bernardino. How much did you tell her about what I'm planning?"

"I don't know anything about your plan."

"Not the right answer, Ernie," said Marriner. "You should've said something like, 'Which of your multitude of plans are you talking about, sir?' You know, you're not even any good at playing dumb."

Shiboo hugged himself to try to control his shivering. "All right, sir, I did hear a few rumors—since I do drop in at your various homes delivering androids—about some plan to team up with certain Tek cartels in Europe."

"Which cartels, Ernie?" He reached over and took hold of the Japanese's wrist.

Grimacing at the pressure on his pudgy wrist, Shiboo answered, "Anzelmo was the only name I heard, sir."

"What exactly are Anzelmo and I and the others working on, Ernie? How much of that did your spying bring out?"

"It wasn't spying," contradicted Shiboo. "After all, I was deeply involved in the Tek trade for years and I'm bound to be interested in some kind of Tek network that may well put every Teklord in America out of business."

Marriner smiled. "Yes, you'd naturally be curious about that," he agreed. "Where's the Bernardino woman?"

"Don't you have her?"

Marriner shook his head and let go of the wrist. "No, although I'd very much like to."

"Then I don't know," said Shiboo. "Listen, sir, I'm really sorry if my curiosity has caused you—"

"Your damned curiosity, putz, has contributed to a lot of people finding out something about my plan."

"As I say, I'm really sorry."

Marriner slid open a drawer in his desk. "And well you should be, Ernie." He lifted out a snub-nosed stungun and shot the Japanese.

⹀ 13 ⹀

JAKE TURNED AWAY from the monitor screen in the white metal wall of the interrogation suite. "Bascom appears to be successfully stalling Lieutenant Drexler," he announced. "But there's no way of telling how long he'll be able to bring that off."

At the center of the circular room the bald Dunkirk was strapped in a padded white metal chair. His eyes were open wide yet he didn't seem to be seeing anything.

Gomez, resting his hand on the arm of the chair, said to the young Chinese woman who was stationed just to the rear of Dunkirk, "Time is on the wing, Terri. Can we commence questioning this *cochino*?"

Terri Lee glanced over at a wall clock. "Okay, Gomez, the truth injection should've taken hold by now. Start slow, huh?"

Leaning closer, Gomez inquired, "You're Nigel Dunkirk?"

The bald man answered, in a slightly droning voice, "You got it, mate."

"Who hired you for this job?"

"Don't know his bloody name."

"Why's that, Nigel?"

"That's the way these things work out," said Dunkirk. "I'm a freelancer, do you see. People know my specialties, know I got a good reputation and a success rate that's blooming miraculous. When they contact me, mate, they like to remain strictly anonymous."

"You know Johnny Trocadero?"

"Heard of the bloke. Never actually met up with him."

"Could he be behind this?"

"He might. He might not."

Frowning, Gomez asked slowly, "Where did you take Jill Bernardino?"

Dunkirk blinked, grimaced. "I'm not supposed to tell."

Terri said, "You have no choice."

"Where did you take her?" repeated Gomez.

"Glendale Sector."

"A little more specific, *por favor.*"

"Hotel Santa Clara."

"A true dump," observed Jake.

"Who'd you turn her over to?"

"Night clerk."

"Name of?"

"Marsh Glendenny."

"A certifiable lout," said Jake.

"*Sí,*" agreed Gomez. Hunching his shoulders, he leaned even closer to the truth serum–drugged Dunkirk. "You were supposed to grab Jeffrey Monkwood too?"

"That's right, mate."

"Same client?"

"Far as I know."

"What's the connection between Monkwood and Jill Bernardino?"

"Well, as I understand it, this bloke was putting the blocks to her, know what I mean?"

"What else?"

"You can search me."

"When you got Monkwood—where were you to take him? Same hotel?"

"No, him we got to drop off at the Sheridan Hotel in the Long Beach Sector."

"Turning him over to who?"

"Charlie Menken. He's the manager."

Gomez asked him, "What about me and my partner?"

"You two blokes we are just going to snuff out."

"We better move along, Sid." Jake nodded at the monitor screen that was showing him what was taking place up in the chief's office. "I don't think Bascom's going to be able to stall the minions of the law much longer."

Stepping back, Gomez said, "Hate to leave you with this *pendejo*, Terri."

"It's okay," she said, smiling. "You and Jake had better scoot out one of our secret exits."

Gomez was handling the controls of the skycar, guiding it through the darkening twilight toward the Glendale Sector of Greater Los Angeles. "Okay, *amigo*," he said, "this is how I see things. On the one side we have these European Teklords who've banded together to pull off something *muy importante* and on the other side there's Johnny Trocadero, notorious local Tek kingpin, and possibly other native Tek luminaries. Somehow Jill got herself caught smack in the middle."

Jake was in the passenger seat, a small reader/scanner held in his hand and a listening bug in his ear.

"*Amigo?*" said his partner after waiting for a response.

"Huh?"

"I was laying out my astute analysis of this whole business—and you thus far have failed to reply. Even polite applause would be appreciated."

"Sorry, Sid." He tugged out the listening bug and tapped the reader/scanner. "Been listening to a transcript of the thoughts that Terri and her crew gleaned from what passes for a brain in Dunkirk's robot."

"*Cosa?*"

Jake touched a key and the voxbox in the reader began speaking. ". . . man on the vidphone screen is a big fellow, tall, hefty, in his fifties. Not too smart, though, not used to doing this sneaky stuff. Look at him, he didn't even think to blank the screen. And we can see part of the room he's in, too. Half of an animated poster showing on the wall. Says *Supp Starv Cent.*"

Jake turned off the little machine. "That's part of the bot's recollections of one of the people who contacted Dunkirk to set up Jill's kidnapping."

"*Dios.*" He gestured at the reader. "That doesn't make sense, Jake."

"Nevertheless, that sure sounds like a description—going by the background file on him I looked over—of Ernst Reinman. And, Sid, he'd sure be likely to have a poster saying *Support the Starvation Center* gracing his wall."

"*Sí*, but why in the hell would Jill's current spouse be involved in arranging her abduction?"

"Could be he was tired of her fooling around."

"Kidnapping is a pretty drastic cure for infidelity."

"Yeah, and besides, we already know several Tek cartels are tangled up in this."

"Later, however, I better," suggested Gomez, "have another chat with the distraught husband."

• • •

From the run-down little park near the old center of the Glendale Sector you had a good view of the Hotel Santa Clara. It was a six-story structure, rising up next to a weedy lot that had once been a complex of tennis courts. Built during the revival of interest in the Spanish style in the early years of the twenty-first century, the Santa Clara had slanting red tile roofs and real wrought-iron bars guarding each and every window.

In the growing twilight Gomez and Jake were crouched behind a stand of real pepper trees. Scattered on the simulated grass were five used Tek chips.

"I don't think much of the public recreation program in this area." Gomez kicked at a chip.

"Be best to surprise the night clerk," said Jake. "Then we can ask him where Jill is."

"Think she could still be inside that *pocilga*?"

"Hard to tell, Sid. The opposition probably already knows we've got Dunkirk," said Jake. "Anyway, I'll head down the alley on the left of the place and let myself in the back way. Once I locate Marsh Glendenny, I'll let you know on the palmphone. Then you—"

"*Momentito.*" Gomez stood up. "Jill, after all, was once related to me by marriage. I'll make the initial assault."

Jake made an okay-by-me gesture with his left hand.

Patting his shoulder holster once, Gomez slipped clear of the park, crossed the street and began strolling, as unobtrusively as possible, toward the Santa Clara.

Before he reached it an immense whomping noise sounded inside the old hotel. The whole structure began to break apart, the red tiles sliding away from each other and spinning and clattering down through the night. The wrought-iron bars flew away from the disintegrating building, turning into twists and zigzags of black. The inside of the hotel mixed with the outside as it all went cascading toward the street.

Immense clouds of black sooty smoke were rolling thickly out of the crumbling, tumbling building.

Jake couldn't see Gomez at all.

— 14 —

Johnny Trocadero said, "Well, I'll be dipped."

Yedra Cortez asked, "That's your only comment, runt?"

Trocadero was thin and about a half-inch shy of being five feet tall. His hair, which was a glittering platinum, he wore in bangs. "You know those slurs about my stature upset me, sweetheart."

"So fire me, shrimp." She was five six, slender, dark and with her hair cropped to a bristly fuzz.

Chuckling, Trocadero dug out a plazpak of SpeedGum from a side pocket of his sinsilk jacket. "You're indispensable," he told her. "At least just now." He shook a caplet of gum into his small palm, popped it into his mouth.

The two of them were in the main dining room of the new nightspot Trocadero was about to open in the San Diego Sector. The decor here was modeled on the forests of India, and the small tables were set out amidst simulated and holographic jungle trees, vines and flowers. Exotic birds perched on high branches and called.

"If I were you, shorty, I'd kick the ass of whoever's responsible for this." She pointed again at the holographic tiger that was slinking, belly low, across the dining room floor in front of them.

As Trocadero chewed his gum, his eyes grew brighter and his cheeks became pinker. "I only kick ass over something important, darling," he reminded her.

"But look at this goddamn tiger—and they're all like this," Yedra said. "It's only a foot long."

"Darned if it isn't."

"Well, maybe you didn't know this, but real tigers are about five, six times longer."

"I was aware of that, darling." He smiled as the miniature tiger disappeared into the shadows beyond a far row of tables. "We'll have them enlarged to the proper size long before we open next week."

"You've already told those peckers to fix them twice."

"They will," he assured her.

"There's also something wrong with the holographic hippos over in the Africa Grill," Yedra told him. "They ought to be fatter."

"We're going to adjust them too." He shook another caplet of SpeedGum into his hand.

"What'd the doctor tell you about gobbling so much of that crap, dink?"

"He works for me, I don't work for him." Trocadero chewed for a moment and then stared up at the ceiling. "You got to admit all those simulated stars up there look terrific."

"There's two Big Dippers." Yedra didn't bother to glance upward. "I'll tell you another thing that . . ." There was a very faint humming sound, which seemed to originate inside her head. "Hold on, shrimp, I'm getting an s-mail message."

Shuddering once, the diminutive Teklord helped himself to more gum. "That would give me the absolute creeps," he commented. "Having a damned phone implanted inside my conk."

"It's not a phone, it's a tiny little mail chip."

He bounced a few times on the balls of his tiny feet. "So what's coming in?"

She made a hush-a-minute motion with her hand. Then she smiled. "The Hotel Santa Clara ceased to exist exactly five and a half minutes ago," she reported.

"I'll be dipped," commented the Teklord. "Austin Quadrill is as good as he claims then." He nodded a few satisfied nods. "Bodes well for what we have in mind for next week."

"I wish you'd stop using words like 'bodes.' "

"Was Marshall Glendenny in the joint when it went up?"

"He was," she replied. "But what's even better news— it's just about certain that a Cosmos op was killed by the explosion."

Trocadero stopped chewing. "Jake Cardigan?"

"The other one. That *lambioso*, Gomez."

Trocadero shrugged his narrow little shoulders. "That's okay," he said, bright eyes going wider. "We'll get him next time."

The wide curved one-way bedroom window afforded a view of the twisting mountain road far below and the shadowy woodlands. Everything out in the night was tinted a pale silvery blue.

"You're really not paying anything like enough attention to me, Professor," complained the naked young woman who was sitting on the edge of the big oval bed and slowly swinging one leg back and forth.

Jeffrey Monkwood said, without turning away from the

window, "You don't have to address me as professor all the time, Annalee."

Annalee Tarkington shrugged her bare shoulders. "It's exciting to do it, though, Professor," she explained. "Sleeping with one of my professors has been my goal ever since I transferred to UC/Venice."

"I'm flattered."

"You should be, I turned down two other profs."

"Fine," he said, still watching the dark distant road.

"You're here more for the hideaway aspects of my parents' number three home than you are for the screwing, obviously," she told him.

"Not many landcars come up this far."

"Very few people come up to this mountaintop enclave by any means of transportation, Professor," Annalee said, stretching out on her back on the wide bed and locking her arms behind her blonde head. "My parents, for example, haven't spent a night here in over three years."

"Are you certain your security system is still functioning properly?"

She brought her knees up. "My parents are even more paranoid than you are," she answered. "This is an extremely secure spot, trust me. Didn't you pay attention to all I had to go through to get us inside?"

He took a few steps away from the window. "I'd better get dressed," he said, still staring out into the night. "I have to make a vidphone call." Frowning, he hurried back to the window, pressed his palm against it and looked out and up. "Skycar flying over."

"They do that now and then."

"Okay, it's okay. The skycar is going on by."

She sat up, watching him. "Was this little anticlimactic tussle we just went through about it for the sex stuff tonight, Professor?"

"Damn it, Annalee, I've got other things on my mind tonight."

"You ought to be worrying more about what a poor performance you gave."

He strode to the bed, took hold of her bare shoulders, shook her. "There are people out there in Greater LA somewhere looking for me—no, *hunting* for me," he said, voice loud. "They may want to kill me."

"Don't yell," she said.

Very gradually, he moved his hands away from her. "We've had a small romance going this semester, Annalee," he said in a voice touched with impatience and annoyance. "When I suddenly needed a place to hide out for a time, I thought of you. You were helpful enough to bring me here and I appreciate that a good deal." He paused, moving back from the bed. "But the sex was your idea."

"It obviously wasn't yours."

Very quickly, even though he paused twice to look out through the one-way plastiglass, Monkwood dressed. "You told me that your father had a tap-proof phone in his den here," he said to the young woman, who still hadn't bothered to put her clothes back on. "Is it working?"

"Everything works, Professor, my parents see to that."

"I have to try to contact somebody."

She gestured, unenthusiastically, toward the door.

The only illumination in the large domed living room came from thin litestrips along the floor. Monkwood hurried through the room and into the den.

"Lights," he said as he crossed the threshold.

The smaller room remained dark.

"Lights," he repeated, making his way to the vidphone on the desk.

Nothing happened.

"The house only recognizes my parents' voices and

mine.'' Annalee was leaning, still naked, in the doorway.
''Lights, please.''

Three floating globes up near the ceiling blossomed.

She smiled. ''See?''

''Thanks,'' he said, dropping down into the desk chair.
He ran his tongue over his upper lip twice, rubbed his hands
together, flexed his shoulders. ''It would be better if you
didn't listen in on this.''

''You really are in trouble, aren't you? This isn't just
some performance to cover up how disappointing you are
in—''

''Go away, Annalee. Please.''

She scratched her right buttock, shrugged. ''I'll wait in
the bedroom.'' A skeptical smile touched her pretty young
face as she turned away.

He waited a full minute or more before punching out the
number.

A pudgy Japanese appeared on the phonescreen, smiling
cordially. ''You've reached the residence of Ernest Shiboo,'' he said. ''How may I help you?''

''Is your phone tap-proof, Ernest?''

''Of course, Professor Monkwood.''

''Listen. They've grabbed Jill—you probably already
know that. I'm not sure who did the job, but it must have
something to do with what Marriner and the overseas Tek
cartels are planning.''

''Mr. Shiboo is away just now, but I will convey this
message to him,'' said the smiling Japanese. ''Is there anything else?''

Monkwood stiffened, pulling back from the screen.
''What the hell are you—''

''I'm the answering android,'' said the replica of Shiboo.
''Apparently you mistook me for my employer. Employer

and creator, I might add. Shiboo's andies are handcrafted, you know, and noted for—"

"Skip the commercial," cut in the angry professor. "Where the hell is Shiboo, the real Shiboo?"

"He's away at the moment. However, any message—"

"Away where? I have to talk to the man."

The android kept on smiling. "Actually, Mr. Shiboo is on vacation."

"Where'd he go?"

Shaking his head, the android said, "I don't know the location, I only know he won't be back in the Greater Los Angeles area for—"

"What about his companion—Herky?"

"Oh, I imagine he's on vacation, too. He and Mr. Shiboo are inseparable, you know."

"Christ," muttered Monkwood. "They've probably got him already."

"What was that?"

"Nothing, never mind."

"I'll tell Mr. Shiboo you phoned—the moment he checks in with me," promised the simulacrum. "Where can he reach you, Professor Monkwood?"

Monkwood hung up, left the chair, headed into the dim-lit living room. "I'm okay, I'm all right," he told himself in a whisper that didn't convey conviction. "They don't know where I am."

From the bedroom Annalee screamed.

⹀15⹀

GOMEZ WAS STRETCHED out on a narrow white table.

Jake eyed him. "So how do you feel?"

"Like *mierda*," spoke his partner.

Gomez' clothes were ragged, smudged with dirt and soot. There were several plaskin bandages on his battered face, and his moustache was singed.

"That's a good sign."

Gomez looked up at the low ceiling of the parked medvan. "That was some explosion, *amigo*. It hit me like . . . *Chihuahua!*" He sat up on the exam table, just now remembering something. "Jill was in that goddamned hotel. Have they found her, Jake?"

"I don't think she was still there, Sid."

"Have they got the robot dogs sniffing the ruins yet?"

"Just starting."

The two detectives were alone in this recovery compartment. The van was sitting near the small park, and police skyvans and emergency rescue vehicles were still arriving outside.

Reaching over, Gomez caught hold of his partner's arm.

"Help me dismount from my slab, *amigo*," he requested. "I'm feeling a mite woozy."

"You're supposed to recline for a while."

"Who told you that—some run-down medibot? No gadget is—"

"This was a human intern, a young lady."

"Oh so? Pretty, was she?"

"Moderately so."

Gomez swung around until his legs were dangling over the table side. "Being unconscious can certainly handicap one's social life," he observed. "Get back to your theory about where Jill is."

"I got to thinking while you were in your trance."

"How long was I out, by the way?"

"About ten minutes or so."

"*Bueno*, continue."

"I just remembered something about the Santa Clara," Jake told him. "Back when we were both cops, that hotel was run by the SoCal Mafia."

"Everybody knew that, *sí*. But they lost control of it years ago."

"Yeah, but at that time the Mafia goons also ran the NecroPlex cemetery." He pointed a thumb in a northerly direction. "NecroPlex is only about a half-mile from here— and there used to be a series of tunnels and passways linking the hotel with that complex of underground vaults and crypts."

"*Es verdad*." Gomez rubbed at a bandage on his temple. "I remember now. They were doing very well with traditional drugs in those days and they'd built a big underground warehouse right in the NecroPlex."

"Drugs would be brought into the hotel and they'd cart them through those passways to their storerooms."

"The International Drug Control Agency even raided the

setup once about—what?—ten, eleven years ago."

"It occurred to me," said Jake, nodding, "that Jill was delivered to this particular hotel so that she could be conveyed to that old underground warehouse."

"It would be a good place to keep somebody hidden," admitted his partner. "Still, *amigo*, if Jill wasn't in the Santa Clara, why destroy the joint?"

"To keep Glendenny quiet, to dead-end anybody who was searching for her."

"Excessive, though. Send all those down-and-out tenants on to glory just to silence one *hombre*?"

"People in the Tek trade aren't noted," Jake reminded him, "for their humanitarianism."

"I know, *sí*." He hunched, frowning. "Probably this is simply an aftereffect of my playing a key role in a very impressive display of pyrotechnics, Jake—but I'm more pessimistic than you are." He tapped his chest with the fingers of his right hand. "I have a feeling she was still inside and that—that she's dead."

"If Jill's in that rubble, Sid, it'll take maybe a day to locate her," Jake said. "I want to check out that old warehouse tonight."

After a few seconds, Gomez said, "We'd better do that."

"Soon as you're feeling somewhat less wobbly, we can—"

"The only place you two bastards are going," announced Lieutenant Drexler as he joined them in the recovery compartment, "is right straight from here to headquarters."

The gold-plated kitten took three tentative steps across the white plastiglass floor. Then it made a thin, metallic meowing noise, took one more faltering step and fell over on its left side.

The small golden body jittered on the workroom floor for several seconds. A thin wisp of grey smoke came puffing out of the dying mechanism's ear. The kitten rattled once more, was still.

"Shit," said the long, thin man who was kneeling a few feet away. "You should've worked a hell of a lot better than that."

Rising, his head shaking ruefully, he went to his workbench and touched three silvery hammers in turn. Choosing the smallest, he returned to where the clockwork kitten lay.

"You're a real damn disappointment to me." He dropped to one knee and began hitting the little gold-plated kitten.

He hit again and again, with long steady strokes.

The body cracked open, spitting out gears and cogs and twists of wire. A small spill of greenish oil went sliding away from the body.

He pursued a cog that had rolled off a few feet. Catching up, he flattened it with several swift blows of the hammer.

Then, taking a slow breath in and out, he rose up again. "Going to have to do a hell of a lot better on the next one."

"Holocall," announced a voice that seemed to come out of the air.

"Who is it?"

"Yedra Cortez."

"That shrike." He frowned. "Okay, put her through."

A circular panel in the workroom floor slid aside and a holographic stage rose up into view.

After pausing to grind one booted foot into the remains of the kitten, the long, thin man sat himself down in a straight-back metal chair facing the platform. "Good evening, Yedra."

"I'm getting closer to finding out where you're actually

located, Austin,'' said the life-size image of the dark, crew-cut young woman. ''All of this bullshit about not letting us know where—''

''What'd your boss think of the—''

''Johnny Trocadero isn't my goddamned *boss*,'' she told him. ''We're *partners*.''

''What'd your partner think of the explosion at the Santa Clara?'' asked Austin Quadrill.

''He thought that you did exactly what we paid you to do,'' she answered. ''The shrimp isn't planning on sending you a bonus.''

Quadrill smiled at the projected Yedra. ''I got the device in there undetected and it went off exactly on time,'' he said, smile widening and then vanishing. ''Are we going ahead with the major project?''

''Yeah. That's why I'm bothering to contact you, Austin.''

He crossed his legs, examined the sole of his boot. After plucking a tiny silver spring free of the sole, he said, ''Do you have a date or a place?''

''We just found out that Marriner and his crew will be meeting with Anzelmo and some of his people next Tuesday.''

''I can have a device ready and planted by then,'' he assured her. ''I would though, Yedra, like to know where this camp meeting is going to occur. You can't tell me?''

''We don't know yet,'' she said, brushing one flat hand over her close-cropped black hair. ''What you have to do is stand by.''

Another quick smile. ''Exactly what I have been doing,'' he said. ''If they're, for instance, meeting on Anzelmo's home ground—someplace in England, say—I have to factor travel time into my calculations.''

"We expect to know by tomorrow."

"I'll talk to you then." He stood up. "Good-bye."

Her image went popping into nothing. The holograph stage sank and the floor covered it over again.

— ≡ 16 ≡—

THE BLACK YOUNG woman, legs spread wide and hands on hips, said, "Halt about there, loot."

Drexler had been in the act of escorting Jake and Gomez along the night street to a police skyvan, when she came striding up to block his progress. "Out of the way, shyster," he told her.

"*Buenas noches*, Georgia," greeted Gomez.

"You ought to get your ass over to the nearest church of your preferred denomination, Gomez," suggested Georgia Petway, "and thank the Lord that the Cosmos Detective Agency has an attorney like me on retainer." Turning her head slightly, she glared at Jake. "And you, Cardigan, when the hell are you intending to grow up?"

"You seem," observed Jake, grinning at her, "to be annoyed at something."

Lieutenant Drexler said, "These two probably do need a lecture, Georgia, but right now I intend to drag them off to the—"

"Nope, wrong," the black attorney told him.

The cop dropped his hands to his sides, clenching his

fists. "You've pulled some strings, haven't you?"

"Damned right," she answered, smiling. "Pulled strings, greased palms, cajoled, harangued and threatened to send a large flock of chickens home to roost." From a pocket in her skirt she took out a wad of faxmemos. "You're obliged to turn both these loons free exactly now, loot."

The police officer, after making an unhappy noise, grabbed the official forms from her hand. Skimming them, he nodded. "So you've even got something on Judge Boyd, huh?"

"I even got something on you, dear heart. Can we say goodnight now?"

Drexler's fingers closed on the documents, wadding them into a crinkled ball. "Okay, but there's something I want to ask them first."

"According to those papers," said Georgia, "you don't have the right to so much as—"

"It's okay," cut in Jake. "We don't want to spoil our reputation for cooperation by running off and leaving Drexler perplexed."

"*Sí*, go ahead and make your inquiry."

"You shouldn't be giving in to him over—"

Drexler said, "You guys know who Professor Jeffrey Monkwood is, don't you?"

Jake answered, "Sure, he's a friend of Jill Bernardino."

"Well," said Lieutenant Drexler, "about an hour ago a police skycar that was patrolling one of the canyons spotted a young lady wandering, buff naked, along one of those twisty roads. She'd been roughed up and wasn't completely coherent—but she told them she'd been with Monkwood up at her parents' joint when somebody broke in and carried the guy off." He paused, eyeing them. "You know anything about that?"

Gomez said, "We've been looking for the professor, too,

Lieutenant. Apparently somebody else found the *hombre* first.''

''Why would they want him?''

''Same reason,'' said Jake, ''that they want Jill Bernardino.''

''Then suppose you tell me how Monkwood's abduction and this explosion here tonight tie together with—''

''Whoa, cease,'' warned Georgia. ''My clients aren't going to talk to you any longer, Drexler.''

''I need to—''

''You need to read over those crumpled-up orders I delivered to you.'' Stepping between the partners, she grabbed an arm of each and started walking them away.

The police lieutenant made another angry noise, but said nothing to stop them.

Anzelmo came shuffling into the paneled meeting room with a flat plyowrapped parcel under his arm. The elderly Teklord was wearing an overcoat, a neofur hat with shaggy earflaps and a red nearwool scarf around his neck. ''Why the hell don't they heat this place?''

Five other people appeared to be sitting around an ornately carved realwood conference table at the room's center. From the row of high, narrow windows you could see foggy central London, although the room was actually elsewhere.

Halting on his slow way to the chair at the table's head, Anzelmo veered and walked over to where a lean, dark man was seated at midtable. ''Maurice, I've been promising you one of my goddamn paintings for—''

''Anzelmo, old friend,'' said Maurice Pettifaux, ''your venerable eyes aren't serving you too well.''

''What the hell are you babbling about?'' He took a few

more steps forward and held the parcel out to the French Teklord.

"I'm in Paris," he explained. "This is a holoprojection you're trying to make a gift to."

From farther down the table a plump young man with curly blond hair said, "You been promising me a picture." He held out a chubby right hand and made a give-me motion with his be-ringed fingers. "Is it one of your landscapes?"

"That's all I paint, Tony."

"So give it to me and you can send Maury another one." Anthony Macri's fat fingers continued to beckon.

"Go ahead," said Pettifaux. "Tony is a devoted admirer of your artistic works."

"Tony is a habitual ass-kisser." Anzelmo hesitated a few seconds, then tossed the parcel in the plump young man's direction.

"Thanks." Macri sprang free of his chair and caught the painting just before it hit the realwood floor.

Anzelmo took off his fur hat and slapped it down on the table as he settled into his chair. "Okay, my eyes aren't so good anymore," he told the five figures at the table. "Let's see some hands—how many of you bastards are really here?"

Macri interrupted his unwrapping of the painting and held up his hand. A very pale and gaunt man also raised his hand.

Hunched slightly forward, eyes squinting, Anzelmo said, "So only Roger Giford and Tony Macri are really in the room. Maurice and Alex Forman and Mrs. Dooley are projections, huh?" He shook his head and his wispy white hair fluttered. "You'd think—with something this important in the works—you bozos could get your butts over here to England and—"

"Before you start one of your rants," cut in Mrs. Dooley, a large, wide redheaded lady, "answer us a few questions, pet."

"We got an agenda to follow and—"

"Better answer her," suggested Pettifaux, seeming to lean back in his chair. "We've talked this over before you showed up."

"How come," asked Mrs. Dooley, "we still don't have any idea where that Bernardino woman is?"

Anzelmo frowned in the direction of her projection, which was a little fuzzy around the edges. "We do know where she is," he said. "Found out a couple hours ago. Some of my people should be closing in on her just about now."

"And," asked Pettifaux, "what about this Professor Monkwood—I understand he's eluded you as well?"

"We've taken care of the professor," Anzelmo assured them.

"This is marvelous," said Macri, who'd gotten the painting unwrapped. "Just look at all these wonderful sheep."

Giford said, "Attend to business, my lad."

Ignoring him, the plump young man said to Anzelmo, "Thank you so very much."

Mrs. Dooley said, "We've also been wondering how many other people there might be who know about what's afoot."

"With the exception of Mrs. Bernardino," Anzelmo told her, "we've tracked down and silenced them all."

"That's what you assured us last week and yet—"

"What we have to talk about now," Anzelmo cut in, "is our upcoming meeting with Marriner."

Pettifaux asked, "Has a date been set?"

Anzelmo nodded. "If you can quit butting in with half-assed questions for a while, I'll explain things. That is, you know, the purpose of this damned get-together.''

"I just love the way you paint sheep," said Macri, chuckling.

— ≣17≣ —

GOMEZ, CLUTCHING A large bouquet of imitation yellow roses, came strolling back to where Jake was waiting for him in a shadowy grove of simulated oak trees. It was an hour or so away from dawn and the sky still held considerable darkness. "All taken care of, *amigo*," he announced. "In case we need the cover."

Nodding, Jake started downhill along the snaking path leading through the field of grass to a small illuminated chapel. "Only going to be good for about ten minutes," he said to his partner.

After sniffing at the big bunch of roses, Gomez said, "Nobody's going to notice that the secsystem is out for this section of the NecroPlex for at least fifteen. Trust me, there was an expert craftsman on the job."

"Make that five minutes," said Jake, grinning.

Above the shingled little chapel, in litetube letters just under two feet high, floated the words *Wee Kirk #17— Another Convenient Entrance to the NecroPlex®.*

In the anteroom of the chapel, side by side beneath a high, narrow stained-plastiglass window, stood a pair of twins. One was human and the other an android simulacrum. They were short, stout and bright blond.

"Good morning, gentlemen, I'm Mr. Collins," said the one whose name tag identified him as *Mr. Collins: I (Humanoid)*. "Allow us to offer our sympathies to you in your time of obvious bereavement."

"Yeah, that goes for me too," said Mr. Collins: II (Android). "It's really tough tiddy when somebody you know croaks."

"Please." Collins: I nudged Collins: II. "I'm really afraid my colleague and sometime stand-in here at Wee Kirk number seventeen is overdue for a visit to our NecroPlex repair shop."

"Too busy for that, chum," said Mr. Collins: II.

Jake produced a plasticard and handed it over to the human member of the duo. "We're here to put these flowers at the burial site of my late uncle," he explained. "This is my Mourner Permit."

The android Mr. Collins reached over to grab the card before his associate got hold of it. "I check all this kind of stuff."

"Poor old Uncle Ethan." Gomez eased closer to the twins.

"Those are," commented the human Collins, "lovely fake roses."

"Well, his uncle was a dear friend of mine and—"

"Hold it, folks. Something's not quite kosher here." The android Collins had placed the permit card against his forehead and that, apparently, was causing his left eye to blink and send out a bright crimson glare.

"What's the trouble?" Mr. Collins: I began, unobtrusively, to slide his hand into his jacket.

"We didn't have time to get a really state-of-the-art fake

permit,'' explained Jake. ''But we were hoping this one would pass muster.''

''*Lo siento*,'' apologized Gomez as he plucked his stungun from out of his bouquet and fired at the human Collins.

Mr. Collins: I caught the beam in his midsection, made a brief gulping noise, sat down on the plaztile floor.

''The security cams are drinking all this in, jerks,'' the android Collins pointed out.

''Not for about another ten minutes, *perrillo*.'' Gomez used the stungun again.

Mr. Collins: II made much more noise than his twin falling over and hitting the floor.

The Reverend Pearly Owlen was waiting for them around the next bend in the underground passway. The android stood motionless in an alcove, tall, pink-cheeked, clad in a yellow suit.

When Gomez and Jake came within range, something inside the andy produced a faint click. ''Good morning to you, brothers,'' he said, coming alive and smiling. ''I'm the Reverend Pearly Owlen, founder and chief preacher of the Nondenominational Church of the Nonspecific Entity.''

''Pleased to meet you again,'' said Gomez, not slowing.

''If you'd drop a little something in the cup, which is electrified and robber-proof, it will do a world of good for . . .''

The partners hurried on.

''That's the fourth Reverend Pearly Owlen we've encountered thus far,'' mentioned Jake.

''Supposedly he has forty-seven sims of himself down here.''

''Here's the cross tunnel we want coming up.''

A litetube sign on the wall announced: *Rustic Cemetery #17. This way →.*

At the end of the next tunnel lay what appeared to be a small old-fashioned country burying ground. It covered a wide rolling hillside that climbed up to a woodland area. It was simulated midday in #17. Birds were warbling in the treetops and flocks of yellow butterflies were flickering amidst the weathered tombstones.

When Gomez stepped, inadvertently, on a grave, harp music started coming out of its headstone.

"Welcome to the grave site of the late Fredric Dillford," said a voxbox. "In just four and a half minutes we'll show you the highlights of Fred's exemplary life."

A panel on the face of the stone slid open to reveal a small vidscreen.

"Born in Bristol, Rhode Island, in 2065, he . . ."

"Top of the hill," said Jake, starting to climb. "That's where the hidden entry's supposed to be."

"Pity we don't have the time to find out more about Fred."

Beneath a holo oak tree was a tombstone that had the name Eldon Barkerage printed on it in gloletters.

Kneeling on one knee, Jake touched a key on the panel at the stone's top.

"Welcome, wayfarers, to the grave site of Eldon Barkerage, rest his soul," droned a voxbox. "Press one for a stirring and heartwarming docudrama detailing Eldon's early life in Alaska. Press two to see him at his office in the ElectroTrivia Corporation's Rio headquarters from 2113 to 2117."

Jake touched 5, 3, 5 and 6.

The gravestone started to slide back and gradually an opening in the hillside appeared.

"Down this ramp to the old warehouse," said Jake.

"Climbing into a grave," complained Gomez, "is not the jolliest way to commence a journey."

—≡ 18 ≡—

SHE SAT UP, shivering, rubbing at her left arm.

They'd used an injection gun on her, several times since she'd been brought here, and there were several sore red splotches on her skin.

Although Jill Bernardino was aware that they'd used some sort of truth drug on her, she had no recollection of what questions she'd been asked or the answers she was compelled to give. The questions, as well as the brainscan they'd done, all had to do with what she'd found out from Ernie Shiboo.

She hadn't been too smart, she realized, to investigate the tip the Japanese had passed along. Not especially bright to get Jeff Monkwood involved either. Still, he'd done some digging on his own and for reasons that had nothing much to do with her.

These people had probably caught up with Jeff by now. Had him stashed someplace and were questioning him about what he knew.

Thinking about the professor, Jill became aware that

she wasn't feeling much concern over him. Well, that was to be expected. They'd been lovers for several months and she was never able to stay interested in anyone much beyond that. Already Jeff didn't mean a hell of a lot to her.

"Awake already, are you?" A husky young man was standing near her cot, looking down on her with concern. "Was I making too much noise?"

Jill told her guard, "No, Buzz. I simply woke up. Nothing to do with you." She rubbed at her arm again.

He pointed. "Arm bothering you, huh, Jill?"

"A little, yes." She swung her feet over and sat on the edge of the cot. She was still wearing the clothes she'd had on when they ran her to ground.

"There won't be any more shots."

"Oh?"

"Mind if I sit here and we talk for a while?"

"No, go ahead."

"Okay, I'll fetch my chair." Buzz went walking back across the vast dim-lit room to the open doorway. Just outside it was the slingchair he occupied during his all-night guard shift. He picked up the chair, carrying it back to her cotside.

"What did you mean about no more injections?" she asked the young man as he settled into the chair.

This room was part of the old warehouse system. There were still twenty or so big neowood crates stacked over in one shadowy corner.

Buzz glanced around, taking in the whole room and the open doorway. Hunching his broad shoulders, he said, "Since we've become friends, Jill, I guess it's okay to tell you. They're finished questioning you."

"Am I going to be moved out of here?"

"Nope, not until after . . ." He stopped talking, looked away again.

"After what, Buzz?"

"There's a . . . Well, an event is coming up and you're going to be kept here until after it's over."

"And then?"

"Oh, they're going to let you go," he assured her. "That was part of the original deal, see."

"What deal is this, Buzz?"

"I can't tell you much more," he said, glancing once more toward the doorway. "But I think somebody was promised that you weren't going to get hurt or anything."

She touched her fingertips to one of the red blotches on her arm. "Who would that somebody be?"

Shaking his head, Buzz asked her, "Can we talk about my problems now? The way we usually do."

"Sure, go ahead," Jill said. "More troubles with Rhonda?"

"The way you say her name—I get the idea you think it's a pretty stupid name."

"No, Rhonda is fine as a name," she said. "But from what you've been telling me about *your* Rhonda, I don't feel that she's the most warmhearted and thoughtful woman in Greater LA."

Resting his hands on his knees, the husky young man leaned forward. "She was different last night—didn't razz me, you know, didn't tell me I was a lunk," he confided. "We went to that new underwater casino off shore in the Venice Sector. She almost treated me decently, Jill."

"She's been sweet to you before," she reminded him. "Usually when she wanted something."

"You don't think that she's really changing, feeling sorry about the way she—" Buzz jumped to his feet and yanked his lazgun out of his shoulder holster. "What the hell do you want, buddy?"

Gomez, bouquet in hand, had appeared in the lighted doorway. He was swaying slightly from side to side. "Trying to find the final wrestling place," he called out loudly in a slurred voice. "No, make that trying to find the final *resting* place of . . ." His voice trailed off and he took a few staggering steps into the warehouse. "What the dickens is his name? Oh, yeah, Earl S. Grosse, my best friend and—"

"Jerk, this isn't part of the NecroPlex setup," Buzz told him, starting to walk toward Gomez. "Get your ass elsewhere, quick."

Jill left the cot, ran, caught him by his gun arm. "Take it easy, relax," she advised. "He's just a harmless mourner who's had a bit too much to drink."

With a fiery roar the silvery shuttlecraft rose up into the grey NorCal dawn, accelerating away from Marriner Mansion #5.

In his private cabin Marriner was saying, "I'm still waiting for those figures, Miles."

The chair next to his was occupied by a highly polished chrome robot. "Coming in now, boss," replied Miles/26 as he tapped at the small computer screen built into the left side of his chest.

"These are the real numbers?" inquired the media tycoon. "Nobody's cooked them?"

"Absolutely accurate."

"Thirteen percent fewer people are using the Marriner electronic home therapy service than are using the Reisberson Group's shitty service."

"Appears to be so, boss."

"Get me Wenzell."

"Wenzell's dead."

"Since when?"

"Day before yesterday." On the vidscreen built into the right side of the robot's chest appeared footage of a plump woman scattering ashes over the Pacific from the cabin of a low-flying black skycar.

"What'd he die from?"

"Stress-induced suicide."

"Wenzell had a chickenshit streak," said Marriner as his private shuttle climbed higher. "That should've been spotted early on. Who ran the last Suitability Scan on the bastard?"

A triop photo of a leathery little man replaced the last rites of Wenzell. "This gonzo—Dr. Watterman."

"Unload him."

"You got it."

"And dump everybody in his department," added Marriner. "Overhaul the screening process we use. Have that asshole in Zurich revise our Suitability procedures."

"Which asshole, boss? Dr. Helfant or Professor Gunderson?"

"The one with the mole right here."

"Oh, that's Dr. Spruill, Ph.D."

"He's the one I want to work on the job," said Marriner. "Set up an interview for twenty-five minutes from now."

"Right you are."

"Where are those damned attendance figures for our Movie Palace satellite?"

"On the screen."

"Shit, what the hell is wrong? We're still eleven point two percent behind our chief rival, that lousy New Hollywood satellite."

"Up from being fourteen point eight the previous week."

"Not good enough, and haven't I told you I don't like excessive optimism in a robot?"

"You have. Sorry, boss."

"Rodriguez can't seem to run the Movie Palace right. Toss him out on—"

"Be better to wait," advised Miles. "Since Rodriguez is the one who's masterminding your upcoming meeting with Anzelmo on the satellite."

"Another thing, Miles—don't keep telling me stuff I already know," warned Marriner. "I'm heading up to the Movie Palace now to talk to him."

"You can fire the bozo *after* your confab with Anzelmo and his thugs."

"I can junk *you* at any time, too," he reminded.

"That's your privilege, sure. But you'll never find another multibot like me."

"Bullshit, the showrooms are overloaded with them," Marriner countered. "How're our software kiosks in Cuba doing?"

"On the—Hold it, boss. Priority call coming through."

The right-hand screen turned red.

"Who the hell is it?"

"Thelma."

"Jesus, I only left her less than a half hour ago."

"This has to do with Jill Bernardino."

"Talk to me, Thel."

The thickset woman appeared on the screen. "One of Anzelmo's toadies—that obsequious Julie—just contacted us," she said. "They've tracked the Bernardino woman to the NecroPlex down in the Glendale Sector of Greater LA."

"And taken care of her?"

"They'll be doing that as soon as they—"

"Don't contact me until she's dead and gone," Marriner told her. "Let's see that Cuba material, Miles."

"Here you go, boss."

— 19 —

GOMEZ AND JAKE had eased to a halt just around the corridor corner from the entry to the underground warehouse complex.

The curly-haired detective had activated his sniffer gadget and was, as near to silently as possible, getting a reading on the nearest warehouse.

After the gadget spoke to him through an earbug, Gomez leaned close to his partner and whispered, "A goon, armed with a lazgun, is sitting in the corridor guarding the door. Door's open and there's nobody in the warehouse proper but one woman. And she could well be Jill."

Nodding, Jake didn't speak.

Gomez slipped the gadget away in a side pocket, retrieved his bouquet from the floor and concealed his stungun back among the fake yellow roses. "As planned," he said. "Back me up."

Jake nodded again as Gomez, his steps becoming wobbly, headed for the bend.

By the time he reached the open doorway there was nobody guarding it. Gomez, walking like a drunken mourner, made his way to the entrance.

There was Jill, alive, sitting on the edge of a cot far across the shadowy warehouse. And there was a hulky lout in a chair talking to her. "That *mujer* can charm just about anybody," he thought as he paused on the threshold.

The guard sensed him, about then. He popped to his feet, spun and pulled out a snub-nosed lazgun. "What the hell do you want, buddy?"

Fingers closing on the stungun hidden in his flowers, Gomez raised his voice. "Trying to find the final wrestling place," he began. "No, make that the final *resting* place of . . ." He left the sentence unfinished, taking in the room through narrowed eyes.

Jill moved her right hand slightly and gave him a very quick nod of recognition behind the guard's back.

Gomez came wobbling into the big room. "What the dickens is his name? Oh, yeah, Earl S. Grosse, my best friend and—"

"Jerk, this isn't part of the NecroPlex setup," the angered guard said, pointing the lazgun at him. "Get your ass elsewhere, quick."

Gomez kept on moving farther into the warehouse.

Jumping up from the narrow cot, Jill tagged after the husky young man. "Take it easy, relax," she told him, getting hold of the arm that held the gun. "He's just a harmless mourner who's had a bit too much to drink."

"That's absolutely true," asserted the detective.

"Turn around and scram. Otherwise I'll cut you in half with this lazgun."

"Hey, no need to get all belligerent. Soon as you show me where my pal Earl is—" Gomez seemed to trip over his own feet at this point.

He fell forward, slid along the neowood floor. "Distract him," he said to Jill.

She obliged by delivering a series of hard punches to Buzz' kidney area.

"Jill, what the hell are you doing?" The guard started to turn to shove her away.

That was when Gomez jerked his stungun free of the fake blossoms, rolled twice to the left and then sat up shooting.

Buzz huffed. His hands started rising up toward his chest, where the stungun beam had hit him.

Then his fingers spread wide and he dropped the lazgun.

Jill sprinted, put a foot in front of his and gave him a helpful push with her hand across his broad back.

The guard tumbled, sprawled, passed out.

"Very helpful," acknowledged Gomez, rising and dusting himself off. "Any more louts or goons in the vicinity, *chiquita?*"

"We still make a pretty good team, don't we?" She moved close to him, kissed him once on the cheek. "Two new guards will come on duty in about fifteen minutes to replace Buzz."

"You and this slumbering oaf are on a first-name basis?"

"He never told me his full and entire name, Sid. Don't tell me you're jealous?"

He took her hand. "Let's vacate our present location," he suggested, pulling her toward the doorway.

"Thanks for rescuing me," she said. "I knew you would."

"Sí," he said. "It's a hobby of mine."

They were, with Jake leading and Gomez and Jill following, heading for an exit from the underground cemetery network.

"We should be about five minutes from this particular way out," said Jake.

This was another formal burying ground the three of them were passing through. The windblown grass, the immense weeping willows and the stately angels who presided over many of the graves were all holographic projections.

Jill shuddered as she hurried along an imitation gravel path. "I almost ended up being buried down here someplace myself."

Moving up to trot along beside her, Gomez asked, "Is that what they were threatening you with?"

"I'm not actually certain, Sid," she answered. "Buzz—the only guard, by the way, I ever had any conversations with—implied they had specific orders *not* to kill me. I'm not sure, though, that I believe him."

"Who gave those orders?"

"That I couldn't find out."

Jake passed a six-foot-high angel whose wings gently flapped. The path forked just beyond that grave and he took the left-hand turn.

Following, Gomez asked his former wife, "You ever hear them mention Johnny Trocadero?"

"Trocadero heads up the San Diego Tek cartel, doesn't he?"

"That's the very *hombre*, yes. Apparently he's eager to expand his holdings," amplified Gomez. "He's likely the *pendejo* who ordered your—Oops."

The sniffer gadget in his pocket had begun to make a faint chirping sound.

"*Momentito*, Jake," he called to his partner, slowing his pace and then stopping next to a simulated black marble tomb.

Jake came back to join him. "Trouble?"

Gomez, head tilted slightly forward, was listening to the

earbug from the gadget. "*Es verdad*," he replied glumly. "Seems we now have a small parade on our tail."

"How many?"

"This thing is picking up emanations from five humans, two andies and—*caramba*. A full half-dozen robot tracking dogs."

"Trocadero's crew must've found out Jill's gone from the warehouse."

Frowning, Gomez said, "If these are local goons, Jake, they're all of them toting British-made weaponry."

"How far behind are they?"

He checked with the sniffer. "Little less than three cemeteries back and catching up fast."

Jake pointed southward. "We know of two other ways to get clear of the NecroPlex," he said. "I'll take one, you and Jill use the other. That'll split up our posse and maybe give us an advantage."

"*Bueno.*"

"Get her to the agency," said Jake. "I'll meet you there soon as I can." Pivoting on his heel, he started away.

= 20 =

THIS CEMETERY THAT they were racing through looked hundreds of years old. The small, low tombstones seemed weathered and leaned at odd angles. At its center stood an old church, made of wood and painted white.

Gomez and Jill were running hard now, zigzagging between the tumbledown gravestones.

When they passed the front steps of the little New England—style church, Jill suddenly stopped, gasping. "Got to rest, Sid," she told him, one hand moving slowly up and down. "Catch my breath, only a minute, please."

"A minute, but *nada más*. We don't want this to be our final resting place." He paused near her, looking back the way they'd come. Then he tugged out the sniffer gadget and checked it. "C'mon, *cara*, the pursuit group did split up when Jake took the less traveled road. But we still have three humans, an andy and four robot hounds on our heels and they're closing the gap."

"Let's go then." Her face was flushed, speckled with perspiration. Her dark hair was tangled. "Damn it, I thought we'd gotten away clear."

"We will, but it's going to take a bit more effort." He took her arm and urged her into motion.

They ran.

Out of this latest cemetery, then along a metal-walled tunnel, then up a slanting ramp that led them to a long imitation marble corridor that was rich with shelves holding hundreds of gilded burial urns.

"I bet if you spent enough time down here," speculated Gomez as they ran, "you'd end up thinking morbid thoughts."

After they entered yet another long metallic tunnel, Jill said, "I hear an odd noise behind us."

"*Sí*, that's the patter of metal feet," he said. "At least one of those damned robot tracking dogs is catching up."

"Sounds like more than one."

Gomez kicked up his pace, sprinting ahead.

He ran around a bend in the tunnel. After running for nearly a minute, he looked back and found that Jill wasn't there anymore.

"*Dios*," he muttered as he stopped and went back.

She was on her hands and knees on the ribbed flooring. Breathing shallowly, shaking her head slowly from side to side. "I stumbled, Sid. Nothing major."

He looked beyond her and then yanked his stungun from its shoulder holster. "Roll over against the wall, Jill."

Coming through the shadows, not more than a hundred yards from them, was a large robot hound. It was a gunmetal color and its plazeyes glowed a fierce red. The mechanical creature's jaw was filled, crowded, with sharp-edged silvery metal teeth.

The metal paws made hollow clattering sounds as, galloping, it narrowed the distance between them. A tiny silver knob protruding from its skull was giving out a continual reedy beeping.

Gomez knelt, knees wide, and swung up his gun. "Stay hunkered," he told the woman.

The robot hound left the floor of the tunnel and launched itself into the air, aiming straight for the fallen Jill.

The beam from Gomez' stunner took it in the chest.

The metallic dog gave a tinny yelp, quivered, dropped to the floor. It got up, though, and starting heading for Jill again.

"Hey, *perro*, this is supposed to stop you in your damned tracks." Gomez fired the stungun once more.

The dog was nearly to Jill, teeth starting to snap. The second beam caused it to swerve, slam into the wall as it lost its balance.

Leaping up, Gomez ran over and shot a third time, standing right above the slowed mechanism.

The hound's teeth made a final try to bite at Jill before it collapsed.

"That's a very strong little *madre*," observed Gomez as he helped her to rise. "Usually you can disable them with one shot from a stungun."

"Thanks again, Sid."

His arm around her, they started away.

The second dog that found them had two men with it.

Gomez was crouched before a narrow metal door at the end of a low tunnel. "I'll get this lock device jobbed in a few more seconds, *chiquita*," he assured her.

"Sid, I think I hear footsteps again." Jill was leaning against the wall, arms folded under her breasts, breathing slowly in and out. "Not just a bot dog either. And coming up fast."

"I hear them, too," he admitted. "But once we get this door open, we'll be in the outside world once more."

The lock gave off a click and then a whir.

"*Bueno*." Gomez nudged the door with his elbow.

It didn't budge for a few seconds, then, with a rusty creaking, it swung open outward. Grey daylight showed.

Jill took his hand and they ran out of the final tunnel and up into a small battered kiosk.

Gomez shut the door behind them.

They stepped out into a large circular public plaza. Three skyvans were parked near its edge and another van was dropping down through the early morning. Copper-plated robots, most of them wearing bright blue overalls and yellow straw hats, were in the process of setting up outdoor food stands and counters. A pretty blonde android in an imitation gingham dress was arranging a display of flowerpots with artificial plants in them.

A pair of robots was sending aloft a floating litesign that proclaimed: *Welcome to the Pasadena Sector Farmers' Market.*

"That's not too bad," commented Gomez as they jogged away from the NecroPlex exit. "To come back from the dead in Pasadena."

"How do we get to the Cosmos Agency?"

They stopped and Gomez scanned the area. "I'm sure one of these rustic lads would allow us to borrow a skyvan."

Back across the plaza the exit door flew free of its hinges, went hopping across the flagstones and smacked over with a clang. Sooty smoke gushed out into the morning and then a heavyset black man hefting a lazrifle lunged into view. Another bot hound, red eyes flashing, followed.

"The blue van," said Gomez, starting to run.

They dodged an overalled robot who was setting plazcartons of hydroponic produce out on a neowood stand. Across the bib of his trousers were the words *Naturally Yours! From Worldwide Drugs & Food.*

A second man, a short blond fellow wearing a checked suit, came up from belowground to join in the pursuit.

Gomez and Jill reached the door of the blue skyvan. It had the familiar *Farmland Enterprises International logo* emblazoned on its side in yellow liteletters.

"In, *bonita*." He gave the woman a boost and then joined her in the cabin.

"Hey there, feller," called a rustic robot. "That there's my buggy."

Paying him no mind, Gomez pulled out a small black tube. He bounded into the pilotseat and touched the tube to the start button.

The skyvan's engine came alive.

At that same instant the door of the cabin was cut clean in half, from top to bottom, by the beam of a lazrifle. The right-hand half fell away.

"We'll relocate," said Gomez, rapidly punching out a takeoff pattern.

The van shook, then began to rise up from the plaza.

The robot hound leaped, caught the bottom edge of the door frame with its metal paws.

Gomez passed his stungun to Jill. "Take care of that *perrito* while I concentrate on stealing this vehicle."

She left the passenger seat, walked closer to the doorway of the cabin and aimed the stungun.

The dog had nearly succeeded in pulling itself into the van.

Jill fired.

The beam hit the robot hound in the forehead. The color faded from its gleaming red eyes. The eyes snapped shut, a faint disappointed whir came out of its skull and it let go. It fell three hundred feet into a wheelbarrow full of simulated corn.

= 21 =

GOMEZ, ONCE AGAIN, left his chair to cross to one of the windows of Bascom's tower office and gaze out into the brightening morning. "*Muy malo*," he said, mostly to himself. "Jake should've been here long since—or contacted us."

Bascom was behind his desk. "Sid, your partner may be unorthodox, but he's capable as hell," he told the uneasy operative. "Jake can take care of himself."

Jill, who was occupying a client chair, reminded, "It's only been a little more than an hour."

"Too long." Gomez headed for the door. "*Jefe*, you can find out what Jill knows and fill us in later."

"If you're going back to the NecroPlex," said the agency chief, "you maybe want to take a couple of other—"

"Right now I'll try it alone." Gomez opened the door. "You can trust Bascom, Jill. More or less."

After he'd departed, Jill said, "You know, Walt, he was probably the best husband I've had so far. Too bad I futzed that up."

"I quit giving advice to the lovelorn several years back,"

Bascom told her. "Suppose you tell me what you know. That should help us keep you alive and aboveground."

Nodding, Jill said, "By the way, I don't especially want to go home just yet. Is there someplace you can put me up—some place safe?"

"Sure, safety is a specialty of Cosmos."

She turned to glance again at the doorway Gomez had gone through. "And can you notify my husband? Tell him I'm okay but won't be coming home for a spell."

"Later today I'll be sending Reinman a full report plus our bill," Bascom said. "Your husband is our client."

"Ernst actually hired you to find me?"

"He did indeed."

"I wouldn't have thought I was that important to him anymore."

"Did you happen to discuss what you found out from Ernie Shiboo with your husband?"

Her eyebrows rose a little. "Oh, you know about Ernie, huh?" she said. "Yes, I did tell Ernst about some of what I was finding out. It helps give the illusion that we still give a shit about each other and what we're up to."

Bascom said, "Here's what I know about Shiboo. He once held an important position with the now defunct Hokori Tek cartel. He went into the android supplying business and has had frequent dealings with Leon Marriner, the media and communications tycoon from NorCal." He paused. "I'm also pretty certain Shiboo's disappeared."

"Kidnapped like me, you mean?"

"Maybe kidnapped," he answered. "Maybe killed."

She took a deep breath. "I've gotten into a lot of messes in my life, Walt," she said.

"I was aware of that, Jill."

"But, Jesus, this is the worst one yet. People are getting killed apparently."

"So tell me what you know about what's going on," he urged, leaning forward and resting both elbows on his desktop.

"You can," she said, "record what I'm going to say."

Bascom smiled a narrow smile. "We've been recording, filming and taping ever since you and Gomez dropped in on me."

She looked up at the ceiling, as though trying to spot concealed cameras and mikes. "Okay, this has to do with Leon Marriner," she began, putting her hands together in her lap. "He . . . well, Marriner and a group of his best technicians have been working for over two years on a system for delivering the same sort of addictive fantasies and escapes that Tek does." Jill twisted her fingers together, frowning. "They apparently perfected this method and they can now do everything Tek does for its addicts, but without any of the paraphernalia. No Brainbox, no headgear and, most important, no Tek chips."

"How does he deliver the stuff then?"

"By way of computers," Jill answered. "They call their systems, among themselves, TekNet. I was trying to get more details when I was grabbed—but what Marriner seems to have come up with is a simple attachment for your computer. You hook that up and you get your Tek fix that way."

"What about side effects?"

"Far as I know, Walt, they're about the same as with Tek chips," said Jill. "Addicts—and you're aware that I'm a reformed Tekhead myself—who use any sort of brainstim electronic drug run the risk of suffering some pretty scary side effects. Anytime you deliver a powerful stimulant directly to your brain, you're going to become an eventual candidate for brain damage, flashbacks, fits and seizures and, in some cases, a complete shutdown of your neural system. That happens and you're dead and done for."

"If they plan to send their Tek dreams by way of computer networks," speculated Bascom, "they're going to be traced and put out of business."

Jill laughed. "C'mon, Walt, we're talking about Leon Marriner here. He used to be the boy genius of computers," she said. "TekNet is going to set up an extremely sophisticated system of defense and diversions. They're figuring it'll take authorities like the International Drug Control Agency at least a year or more to even come anywhere near them."

"I suppose Marriner can do that if anybody can."

"And in two years, considering that there are a hell of a lot of Tek addicts all over the world—hell, Marriner and his group can pull in billions of dollars."

The agency head murmured agreement. Then he said, "Apparently, to cover his backside, Marriner is planning to go into business with some of the Teklords themselves."

"He is, yes." Jill shifted in her chair, crossing her legs, then uncrossing them. "According to what Ernie Shiboo originally told me—and adding what I was able to dig up on my own—Marriner formed a partnership with Anzelmo."

"The top Teklord in England."

"Anzelmo formed a group of other imprint Tek cartel heads and they went in on TekNet," Jill continued. "Anzelmo's group took care of about half the financing of the research."

"If TekNet actually works and gets rolling," speculated Bascom, "it could put most of the lads who deal in the traditional Tek chips out of business. Or at least cut their profits way down."

"I suspect that the people who grabbed me may've been rivals of the Marriner/Anzelmo combine."

"Johnny Trocadero is probably the fellow who had you kidnapped," said the Cosmos chief. "Not to silence you, which is what the Anzelmo faction would want, but to find out all you know about the TekNet operation."

"Anzelmo's people must be the ones who came after us down in the NecroPlex," she said. "I got the feeling they weren't chasing me just to ask questions." She rubbed, slowly, at the red splotches on her bare arm. "I'm still in a whole stewpot of trouble, Walt."

"Yes."

After a few silent seconds, Jill said, "On my own, following up on Shiboo's tip, I found out that Marriner and Anzelmo are going to have a meeting soon. They plan to get-together to work out the final details for launching TekNet."

"Any specifics on that get-together?"

"I only know it's scheduled to take place within a few days," Jill replied. "The reason I was stupid enough to let myself get lured to the old Hollywood Starwalk Park the other night was because an informant had promised me more information on the damned meet."

Bascom leaned back in his chair. "In addition to your husband—you also told Professor Monkwood about TekNet, didn't you?"

"Yes, and Jeff decided to do some digging on his own."

"A dangerous idea."

"He's almost always in need of money," she explained. "I think he was hoping to find out something he could sell to somebody—or use for blackmail purposes." She looked up, directly at the agency chief. "Has something happened to Jeff?"

"Nobody is clear as yet what the professor's fate is," he said. "But he was grabbed while he was shacking up with one of his lady students."

''Poor Jeff.''

Bascom eyed her. ''Doesn't sound as though you're too concerned. I note a certain lack of sympathy and empathy both.''

''I tend to get tired of people fairly fast, Walt, and lose interest in them,'' Jill admitted. ''Didn't Sid tell you that?''

— 22 —

DAN CARDIGAN WENT hurrying along the second-level corridor of the SoCal State Police Academy. When he was still three paces from the metal door marked *Background & ID*, it whispered open.

"C'mon in, kiddo." The large, wide copper-plated robot who managed the setup was rising up out of his wicker rocker. "Got some deepdish trouble, huh?"

"How'd you know about—"

"I told him." Molly Fine was standing just to the rear of the big robot's chair. She was a slim, dark-haired girl, a year older than Dan.

"So you're cutting our Field Forensics 6B class, too?" The door hissed shut behind him.

"This is more important," she told him. "And you keep forgetting that we're a team."

"So far I haven't been able to come up with anything useful about your pop," said Rex/GK30. One wall of the big room was filled with rows of infoscreens, and the coppery bot gestured at it now. "Nothing's come up from any of the conventional sources as to where the heck he might be.''

''We don't want just *conventional* sources, Rex,'' the young man told him. ''Something's happened to my dad and—''

''Why not contact Bascom at Cosmos again?'' suggested Molly.

''Did that on my palmphone ten minutes ago,'' he told her, shaking his head. ''There's still no word.''

''It could be,'' she said, putting a hand on his shoulder, ''that Jake's just following up on something and—''

''Nope, we've already gone over that possibility, Molly,'' said Dan. ''It's two-eleven in the afternoon. He would've gotten in touch with somebody by now.''

''Jake Cardigan is one tough bozo,'' reminded the bot. ''He can take care of himself. Maybe you ought to relax and—''

''I want to try Gomez again,'' said Dan, impatient. ''I haven't been able to contact him all day.''

''He's supposed to be out hunting for your father, isn't he?'' asked Molly.

''Yeah, and if anybody can find him, it'll be Gomez.''

The robot lumbered over to a bank of vidphones, punched out a number on one of them with a thick coppery forefinger.

The phonescreen remained blank for nearly half a minute.

Then Gomez's face appeared. ''*Sí?*''

Dan ran over to the phone. ''Sid, it's me.''

''*Buenos días*,'' said the curly-haired detective. Behind him you could see a stretch of bright-afternoon Pacific and the tops of a few imitation palm trees.

''Have you found my dad?''

''Not yet, *niño*,'' answered Gomez. ''However, I did

manage to unearth some information on my return trip to the NecroPlex. I'm in the process of following up on that."

"Is he alive? Is he okay?"

"Let's assume he is," said Gomez. "What I found out is how those *pendejos* got into that underground complex. Unlike Jake and me, they bribed their way inside. I located the guard they utilized and persuaded him to provide me the name of the *cabrón* who sent them to him with cash in hand."

"Who is it?"

"A *gordito* who calls himself Sir Denis Rowley," replied the detective. "Took me this long to track him down to his current hangout—a ragtag bistro here in the Hermosa Beach Sector of Greater LA. Dump known as the Khyber Pass Pub and Dance Pavilion."

"I could come down there and help you to—"

"No." Gomez held up his hand, shaking it negatively. "We're dealing with some very dangerous *hombres*, Dan."

Reluctantly, Dan said, "Okay, I'll stay on the sidelines for now. But, Sid, please—let me know what you find out."

"*Por supuesto.* Of course," promised Gomez, and signed off.

When the android stepped on his left foot for the third time, Gomez muttered, "*Caramba.*"

"Nix," whispered the pretty platinum-blonde andy the detective was waltzing with. "If you draw attention to my clumsiness, it's going to be the scrap heap for yours truly, mister."

"Is it okay if I grimace?"

"I suppose, so long as you do it subtly."

There were only seven or eight couples waltzing around

the large oval dance floor of the Khyber Pass Pub and
Dance Pavilion.

Gomez was scanning the swirling clientele and also
watching the arched open doorway that led into the public
house section. "Let's return to my earlier inquiry, Mitzi."

"About Sir Denis, you mean?"

"The very *hombre* I'm interested in."

"Well, he—" She ceased moving, eyes going blank.

The music had stopped and with it all the female dancing
androids.

Sighing, Gomez fished out his Banx card and inserted it
into the thin slot between the pretty android's breasts.

"Where was I?" She blinked as another waltz came blar-
ing out of the array of ceiling speakers.

"Sir Denis," prompted Gomez.

"Oh, sure. He's here every afternoon." Mitzi nodded in
the direction of the arched doorway.

"So he's here now?"

"Funny." She frowned.

"What's funny, *chiquita*?"

"Oh, that he's really late."

"Usually comes in at a certain time, does he?"

"Right, always at one-thirty p.m. Prompt."

Nodding, Gomez asked her, "Any notion where he resides or—Ouch."

"Oops, sorry."

"Where does Sir Denis live?"

"Near here."

"*Bueno*," he said. "How about a few more details—
street address and the like?"

"Far as I know, he—" The music stopped, Mitzi froze
again.

Gomez whipped out the Banx card and thrust it into the
slot.

"What say we sit this one out?" she suggested. "My dogs are aching." The pretty blonde android took his hand and led him over to one of the small rickety tables in a shadowy corner.

"About Sir Denis's present location?"

"Well, the last time I danced with him—and if you really want to get your tootsies stomped on, try waltzing with a fat man," she said, elbows on the tabletop. "Anyway, the last time I talked with the guy, he told me he had rooms down at the Chesterton Hotel."

"*Gracias.*" Gomez started to stand up.

A heavy hand grabbed his shoulder from behind and shoved him back down. "What's the rush, Sherlock?"

— 23 —

SLIGHTLY HUNCHED, HANDS in his trouser pockets, Marriner stood at a wide viewindow in his suite in the Movie Palace Casino Hotel. The number of wrinkles on his black forehead kept increasing as he gazed down at the main street of the simulated city that existed within the orbiting satellite. "Get Swanson," he said without turning from the window.

Miles/26, his chrome chest glittering in the artificial sunlight that was coming in through the multiple windows, was reclining on a low ebony sofa. Feet up, metallic hands locked behind his chrome-plated skull. "Can't do, boss."

"Don't tell me he's dead, too?"

"Nope, Swanson did a flit."

"Where to?"

"He's now working on the New Hollywood satellite."

Marriner said, "See that Swanson has an accident."

"How serious?"

"Your choice, Miles."

"Righto, boss."

145

"So who's responsible for the palm trees down there on Marriner Drive?"

"A lady named Rosebud Semovich."

"Tell her the fronds aren't green enough."

"You got it."

Marriner left the window. "Where the hell is Rodriguez?"

"Ascending in elevator number five."

"He's late."

"By three minutes and seventeen seconds, yes."

Marriner's hands fisted. "Rodriguez better handle our Tuesday meet with Anzelmo and his toadies better than he manages his time."

"I wouldn't, boss, allude to Anzelmo's associates as toadies."

"What *you* call them is your own damn business, but don't—"

"They are all, each in his own way, important Teklords. Cream of the European crop," reminded the mechanical man. "And, more to the point, they're your business partners on the TekNet venture."

Marriner laughed a very quick laugh. "For now," he told the robot.

The pretty blonde android pressed her fingertips to the slot between her breasts. "Gee, Leo, what are you doing to my date?"

The big, wide man who'd come up behind Gomez told her, "Go away now, Mitzi."

"He's a nice guy, Leo, and a paying customer to—"

"Leave us."

"No need to speak to the lady in such a tone," said Gomez in a voice he hoped sounded timid. He was being held in his chair by the pressure Leo was exerting on his shoulder.

"Well, I guess," said the mechanical blonde, getting up from the wobbly little table, "I'll leave you boys. Nice meeting you, mister."

Leo leaned closer. "What you didn't know, Gomez," he said, "is that we got all our andy dancers bugged."

"I am merely trying, sir, to locate my old school chum, Sir Denis Rowley, who—"

"We also got a great monitoring system," continued the dance hall manager. "When I spotted you whirling about the floor with Mitzi, I exclaimed, 'Why, I do believe that's that son of a bitch from the goddamned Cosmos Detective Agency.'"

"That is one of my aliases, *sí*."

"We don't like private dicks hanging around here," Leo explained, bending closer. "Nor are we fond of snoops who're interested in Sir Denis."

Gomez suddenly went slack and slumped in his chair.

That caused Leo to go lurching forward, loosening his grip.

Straightening up, Gomez brought up both booted feet and kicked the underside of the little table.

The table left the floor, went looping upward and then smacked into Leo's head.

Gomez had, meantime, thrown himself to the floor. He rolled twice to his right, executed a reverse somersault that brought him to his feet with his stungun in his hand. *"Adios, cabrón,"* he said to the manager as he squeezed the trigger.

The beam smacked Leo in the groin. He yowled, half turned, crouched, fell to one knee and passed out.

By the time the big, wide man had smacked the dance floor, Gomez was halfway to the exit.

"See you again sometime, maybe?" called Mitzi when he went diving out into the afternoon street.

Gomez holstered his gun and kept running for a good two blocks.

Austin Quadrill allowed himself to smile.

"Much better," he murmured, crouching to pick the silver kitten up from his workshop floor.

The little clockwork animal began purring as he lifted it up close to his face. With one glittering metallic paw it poked at his chin as he inspected it.

"Jesus, that's damn touching," observed a disdainful voice behind him.

He spun around, set the clockwork kitten on a worktable. "Why are you here, Yedra?"

The crew-cut young woman laughed. "Aren't you more interested in the *how* of it, Austin?"

"I assume somebody betrayed me. Gave you my location," he said, scowling at her. "It won't be difficult to find out who."

"And I had to get by your security system too." Yedra laughed again, moving nearer to him. "I told you I'd find you, asshole, and I did it."

"Yes, you can't seem to resist a challenge like that," he commented. "A pity."

She started to reach out to pat the clockwork kitten. "That's damned cute. You ought—"

"I don't want you here." Quadrill caught her wrist before her fingertips reached the kitten. "I don't want anybody here."

She pulled free of him, backed off. "C'mon, *pendejo*, admit that you're impressed by me," she coaxed. "You also, maybe, ought to be a little bit scared, Austin. If you were to screw up on a job for me—hell, I'd come and find you no matter where you were holed up.''

Head slightly tilted to the left, he eyed her. ''Where's the meeting between Marriner and Anzelmo's crew going to take place? That is what you came to tell me, isn't it?''

Smiling, she nodded and ran the flat of her hand over her close-cropped dark hair. ''You still want to work for me? You're not offended that I invaded your privacy?''

''I'm working for Johnny Trocadero *and* you,'' he corrected. ''Soon as you put another third of my fee into my undercover account, I'll get rolling.''

''It's there already,'' she assured him. ''The place is so obvious, we should've guessed it.'' She made an upward jabbing motion with her right thumb. ''Up in the Movie Palace.''

''And it's still Tuesday?''

''Tuesday, just after dinner—satellite time.''

''All right.'' He turned his back on her, tapped the kitten's shiny back with his forefinger. ''I'll take care of it.''

''You sure you can? There's a hell of a lot of security to get through.''

Facing her, Quadrill said, ''I'll do it.''

''Keep in mind, Austin, that I got in here. Maybe you're slipping and we need—''

''I was too complacent about my security,'' he told her. ''Your break-in was just the stimulus I needed.''

She ran her hand over her hair again. ''Okay,'' she said, slowly. ''If anything changes, you'll hear from me.''

''Not in person,'' he said.

Yedra smiled at him. ''I won't scare you again,'' she said.

He took her arm and guided her toward the doorway. ''You've got one of those foolish skull-mail implants, don't you?''

":Yes—and it isn't foolish."

Reaching out, he tapped the door and it slid aside. "Causes you a lot of headaches, doesn't it?"

"No, nothing like that." Yedra stepped out into the hallway. "I never feel any pain from it at all."

The door shut on her and Quadrill returned to his worktable. "You will," he promised quietly.

—=24=—

GOMEZ ENCOUNTERED HIM in an alley.

This particular alley, narrow and unkempt, ran along the backside of the three-story Hotel Chesterton.

The detective was approaching the rear entrance to the tumbledown neostucco building.

Sir Denis Rowley was a flabby man of middle years. His shaggy hair was a carroty orange, his puffy face of a greyish hue. Everything he owned at the moment, he was carrying in one modest-sized suitcase.

He came hurrying, puffing, out of the rear doorway of the Chesterton about ten seconds before Gomez reached it.

"*Momentito*, Sir Denis," Gomez called.

The fat man was waddling off in the opposite direction. "In a frightful hurry, old man," he said over his shoulder.

Sprinting, Gomez caught up with him, grabbed one flabby arm and halted his retreat. "I want to have a small little talk with you."

"Afraid I don't know you, old boy," he said, trying to break away. "No time to chitchat with anyone actually."

"You know me, Denny." Gomez yanked him around so

151

that they were facing each other. "I knew you even before your knighthood."

Sir Denis's eyes narrowed. "Jove, I do believe it's Sidney Gomez," he said. "Forgive me, Sidney, old fellow, but I've a most urgent appointment elsewhere."

"No, actually you're going to tell me where they took Jake."

Sir Denis inquired, "Which Jake would this be?"

From his shoulder holster Gomez yanked his stungun. He jabbed it into the flabby man's middle. "Explain to me who hired you to arrange their entry into the NecroPlex," he suggested, "or you'll suffer from numb *cojones* for the foreseeable future."

"Sidney, you know my code of ethics won't—"

"Who paid you?" he said. "And where is Jake Cardigan?"

The flabby man was perspiring. "English chaps, they were," he said finally.

Gomez prodded with the gun barrel. "And?"

"These are powerful people, Sidney. Mean-minded too, and they aren't awfully fond of a snitch."

"Who?"

Sir Denis swallowed twice, glancing around the alley, uneasy. "They work for the Anzelmo cartel. The only name I know is that of the head chap—Edmond Yates."

"Why did they go into that underground setup?"

"To fetch your wife—that is, your one-time wife," the fat man told him.

"What were they supposed to do with her?"

"Don't know, Sidney." He shook his head vigorously.

"And what were their orders concerning Jake and me?"

Sir Denis glanced around again. "Beastly hot in this alley, don't you think?"

"What were their orders?"

"This they didn't confide in me," he said. "However, old man, I heard—and this is only hearsay, mind you—they grabbed your partner down there. Took him to Doc Sears."

Pulling back his gun hand, Gomez stepped backwards. "That old quack over in the Venice Sector?"

"Fancies himself a therapist," answered the flabby man. "Specializes in mindwipes, brainscans and other shady practices. Used to be a Tek runner, I do believe."

"Okay, Sir Denis," said Gomez, starting to put his stungun away. "You can trot along and—"

"Bloody hell." The fat man was looking up into the hot, hazy sky overhead. "It's too damned late."

". . . wise decision, Jake, to have yourself committed here. Don't you?"

Jake suddenly became aware of himself again.

"Is something wrong, Jake?"

He was sitting in a comfortable chair on a sun-bright patio. Beyond the oval of simulated red brick stretched a broad slanting lawn. Then came woods, tall trees and deep shadows.

Far off, down near the edge of the forest, there were people. Five or six of them, small in the distance, blurred. Walking some of them, one sitting slumped in an electronic wheelchair.

"Jake?"

The woman was sitting a few feet away from him, in a less comfortable chair. She was thin, pale blonde, wearing a buff-colored skirtsuit. Jake had never seen her before.

"I'm sorry, Dr. Weatherford, I didn't quite catch your question," he said to her.

She smiled. "Nothing to be sorry about." She was sitting very straight in the metal chair, hands folded in her lap. "I was simply complimenting you on your decision to come to The Institute—voluntarily—and begin to work on your problem.''

Far downhill one of the tiny figures left the group and went running toward the forest. He suddenly hit some invisible barrier, seemed to hang in the air for a few seconds before dropping to his knees on the bright green grass.

Jake nodded. ''Yes, I realized, doctor, that it was time to do something. My obsession with the death of Beth Kittridge was interfering with my work.''

''With your entire life,'' added the doctor.

''Exactly, yeah. And, I feel, in the time I've been here at The Institute I've started to make progress.'' Jake couldn't seem to remember exactly how long he'd actually been here. He wasn't, he now realized, sure where *here* was.

Dr. Weatherford leaned forward, resting her hands on her knees. ''I know you have very strong feelings about Tek,'' she said. ''Strongly negative attitudes.''

''Getting hooked on Tek screwed up my life.''

She nodded with sympathy. ''I can understand that, Jake,'' she said. ''However, I think a technique we've developed here at The Institute might very well help you to distance yourself from Beth's death.''

He frowned. ''This new technique—it involves Tek?''

''It does,'' replied the thin doctor. ''You have my word, however, that we only use it in a well-controlled and completely safe manner.''

''I don't,'' he said, ''know.''

''Dr. Allensky has had a great deal of success recently with Tek therapy.''

Jake couldn't remember who Dr. Allensky was. ''Well, if he says it works, I suppose it's okay.''

"That's the sort of positive attitude I'm pleased to see you adopting, Jake."

"I came here to work on my problem," he told the therapist. "I'll go along with whatever you and Dr. Allensky suggest."

Smiling, she rose from her chair. "That ends our session for this afternoon," she informed him. "If we can arrange it, I'd very much like to have your first Tek therapy session this evening after the shift one dinner hour."

"That would be fine." He eased up out of his chair and turned away from the doctor.

This wing of The Institute was constructed chiefly of opaque plastiglass panels and silvery metal struts.

He said good-bye to Dr. Weatherford and went walking toward a door marked *Patients' Entrance 6*.

Jake felt that he shouldn't have any notion where his room was. But he did seem to know.

He crossed over to Ramp 3, let it carry him up to Level 5. His room was #5R, and as soon as it scanned his hand print, it let him in.

He crossed the threshold, entering the blue and white room. The door shut behind him.

A concealed voxbox announced, "This is your mantra for this afternoon, Jake."

He sat down in a comfortable blue chair.

The voxbox continued, "Say this one hundred times, Jake. 'I am *not* responsible for the death of Beth Kittridge.' "

Jake nodded. "I am *not* responsible for the death of Beth Kittridge. I am *not* responsible for the death of Beth Kittridge. I am *not* responsible for . . ."

⸗25⸗

SIR DENIS POINTED a fat finger skyward. "Blimey, it's them," he cried, turning a paler shade of grey.

"*Vámonos,*" suggested Gomez, eyes on the dark blue skycar that was dropping down through the smog-heavy afternoon.

Pivoting, Gomez went running along the alley toward the rear entrance to the Hotel Chesterton.

"Bloody hell! They must know you made me shoot off my mouth." The flabby man began a waddling run toward the safety of the hotel.

But he moved much too slowly to escape what the men in the rapidly descending skycar had in mind for him.

The beam of a lazgun came sizzling down. It found him easily, swiftly slicing him clean in half, from left to right, across the middle.

Sir Denis had been able to cry out a few words to express the brief, intense pain he felt. He used his own voice, all trace of British accent gone.

"*Dios.*" Gomez dived into the hotel as the remains of

the fat man slapped and spilled all across the narrow alley-
way.

The detective was in a small, dingy foyer. He spotted a
down ramp and ran for it.

At the bottom of that he found the entryways to three
forking corridors. He took the middle one, jogging into dim
light and borders of deep shadow.

"Let's see if we can," he urged himself, "avoid getting
dismantled."

"Well, it's the greaser." Sitting slumped in an alcove,
with a dented Brainbox resting on her narrow lap, was a
skinny red-haired girl in her teens.

He recognized the emerald and crimson snakes tattooed
on her thin bare arms. "*Chiquita,*" he said, stopping. "We
met the other evening at the Hollywood Starwalk Park.
What are you doing in this—"

"Hey, this is another one of my hangouts."

He pointed his thumb in the direction from which he'd
come. "You know another way out of this joint?"

"Sure."

"Show me?"

She made a chuckling sound and, swaying slightly,
started to stand. "Hell, sure, you saved my ass the other
night," she said. "Who's after you?"

"Some homicidal *hombres.*"

She quickly stowed her Tek gear in the raggedy backpack strapped to her narrow back. "C'mon, greaser," she
invited. "I'll get your butt clear of here."

A lot of unsettling noise was starting to come from
above.

"You some kind of cop?" she asked him as they ran,
side by side, along the twisting corridor.

"Private." He looked back over his shoulder, saw that,
thus far, nobody was following.

"My name is Snooky."

"I doubt that."

"No, asshole, I mean it's my nickname."

"Pleased to meet you, Snooky."

"So who the frig are you?"

"Gomez."

"Typical greaseball name."

"It is that, *sí*," he admitted. "Still, to me, it has more zing than Snooky."

"Up yours then."

"Gracias." He took another backwards look. "Damn, one of them is tailing us now."

About two hundred yards back in the shadowy corridor a big bald man was trotting. He swung a lazrifle in his right fist.

"Relax, Gomez," advised Snooky. "We're almost safe."

"Stop right there," called the bald man. "Else you're both dead and done for."

There were seven other patients seated around the dinner table in Patients' Commissary 6. Jake had no recollection of ever having seen any of them before.

But they all, apparently, knew him and as he seated himself in his assigned chair, they nodded or voiced greetings.

"Hi, Bob," he said to the big grey-haired man on his right.

"Better," Bob said.

"How's that?"

"Better," repeated Bob.

"He means," explained the lean blond man on Jake's left, "that he's feeling a lot better. I'm not hearing that, but why argue? Even though Bob seems worse."

"And how are you doing, Mike?" inquired Jake.

"No worse."

One of the two women in the group was a thin redhead in her late fifties. "I looked up your first name, Jake, and do you know what it originally—"

"Holy Jesus, not that what-your-name-means crap," complained the heavyset black man opposite her. "She does that with every new guy who comes along the pike."

"I simply feel," said Ann, "that people like to know stuff like that. It's interesting."

"It is," Jake assured her.

"Here comes the first two courses," observed Mike.

A pair of servobots had come rolling into the small, yellow-walled dining room. One was pushing a cart that held a large plastiglass soup tureen, the other carried a tray with eight small bowls of salad upon it.

"Bet it's cream of tofu tonight," said the black man.

"Naw, this is Sunday," reminded Mike. "Sunday is always, eternally, meatless chowder."

The black man frowned. "You sure, absolutely, that this is Sunday?"

"Didn't we begin the day with church?" Mike reminded as the bot ladled out a bowl of soup. "Yep, it's chowder."

"Chowder's always lousy," mentioned Bob, picking up his soup spoon.

"Your salad, sir." The other robot was bent close to Jake. "You'll be having a visitor right after dinner," it informed him in a thin whisper.

Not acknowledging the message, Jake tried his salad.

A faint humming began coming from the blue wall of Jake's room.

He stopped repeating his evening mantra and moved free of his chair.

Very quietly, a panel in the wall slid aside.

There was a middle-sized man in his early sixties standing in the recess behind the panel. "Don't worry, Cardigan," the visitor said as he stepped out of the wall. "I've rigged the secsystem. Nobody'll know about this little visit."

He came closer, walking with a slight limp.

Jake eyed him. "You I don't know," he told him.

"Right, because they didn't rig your brain to recognize me and think you've known me for a while." Sitting on the edge of Jake's cot, he tugged up his left trouser leg to rub at the polished chrome leg beneath. "Souvenir of the Brazil Wars. I'm Andrew Simmonds."

Jake frowned, rubbed at the spot between his eyebrows. "Most of today," he said slowly, "I've been getting the feeling that my memories of this place are—well, false."

"They did a rush job on you, Cardigan. And it doesn't seem to be taking that well."

Jake said, "Andrew Simmonds. Sure, I never met you but I know you're with the Office of Clandestine Operations. You are, aren't you?"

His visitor answered, "Very good, Cardigan. You weren't supposed to remember that either."

"They did some kind of mindwipe on me, huh? To make me forget what I was working on—to convince me I was a voluntary patient here."

Simmonds told him, "As I say, they did it in a hurry—in the field. I'd guess it'll wear off before too long."

"Why did they—"

"They want you out of the way for a week or so," he said, massaging his metal leg. "But since you're an important Cosmos operative, they don't want to risk killing you."

"Who are we talking about, Simmonds?"

"A combine of extremely influential people. I'll give you

the details when we have more time," he said. "Oh, and I'm not with the OCO any longer. In fact, I'm supposed to be a patient here." He smiled. "But I've been able to modify my situation some."

"Where exactly is The Institute?"

"Connecticut. That forest you may've noticed outside is Wilderness Preserve number seventeen."

Jake eyed him for a few silent seconds. "And why this visit?"

The former government agent held his voxwatch to his ear. "They'll be coming to take you to your Tek therapy session any minute now, Cardigan," he said. "What I want to know is simple. If I help spring you—will Bascom pay me a fat fee?" He swung off the bed, limped toward the opening in the wall. "Enough for me to buy myself a new identity and lifelong safety?"

"Sure," said Jake. "When can—"

"Later." Simmonds stepped back into the wall and the panel slid shut.

— 26 —

THE BALD MAN with the lazrifle stopped in the corridor. Standing wide-legged, he brought up the gun and aimed it at the running detective.

"C'mon, we'll leave now." The red-haired girl gave Gomez a sudden shove with shoulder and hip.

"Chihuahua," he said as he slammed into a neometal panel.

Snooky threw herself against the same wide panel, also slapping it high up with the palm of her hand.

The wall clicked, the panel flapped open inward.

Behind them the lazrifle crackled.

Gomez, the girl clinging now to his arm, tumbled into darkness.

He regained his balance as the wall shut behind them.

"Hold it a sec, greaser," the girl advised.

Her backpack made some rattling noises and then a small literod clicked on in her skinny right hand.

There was a dirty ramp twisting downward just in front of them.

"We'll scoot along here," she explained, tugging at him.

163

"I know a place we can come up about two frigging blocks from here."

They ran.

It was a cold grey morning in Berlin and Beth Kittridge was alive again.

Slim, pretty, she stepped out of the landcar near the side entrance of the World Drug Court on Potsdamerplatz. She was accompanied by Agents Neal and Griggs of the International Drug Control Agency.

There were ten armed guards, human and robot, lining each side of the long passway from the curb to the narrow entry gate. All around them, huddling under dark umbrellas, a small crowd of curious onlookers had gathered.

Beth was only a few steps from the car when she saw Jake.

He was pushing his way through the bystanders, waving, trying to attract her attention.

"Beth!" he called, grinning his familiar grin. "Thought for a while I wasn't going to make it."

"Jake!" Her smile turned into a pleased laugh. She pulled free of the grip of Agent Griggs, ran the fifteen feet to where he stood. "My God, what happened to you?"

"Long story."

A uniformed Berlin policeman was standing between Jake and the young woman, warning him back with his drawn stungun.

"It's all right, Officer," she said. "He's okay. I know him. Please stand aside."

"I'm sorry, Miss Kittridge." He held out his free hand and gently pushed her back.

"Jake, I was so damned worried," she said around the cop. "Where were you?"

"Gomez and I ran into some extra trouble. Tell you about it later. You okay?"

"I'm fine—now." Using her elbow, she started to nudge the officer out of the way.

"Beth, wait a minute." Agent Neal had come trotting over. He reached out to grab her.

"Oh, really, Emmett." She eluded him, pushed around the policeman. She put her arms around Jake. "I'm so glad—"

There was an enormous explosion.

Then everything froze. Just as the explosives that had been inside the android simulacrum of Jake started to rip the body of the young woman to pieces. An immense silence filled the grey-morning street; the rain ceased falling.

Jake was there now. Himself, not a goddamned kamikaze android sent by the Teklords to destroy the woman he loved. They had to kill her, to keep her from testifying.

But maybe he had a chance to stop that.

He walked up to the two of them, to Beth and the sim.

"Oh, Jesus," he said, starting to cry. "I'm too late. Too late again."

Then everything started up again and he had to stand there and watch what happened to Beth. Blood splashed all over him.

Screaming. Cries of pain. Noise came rolling over him, the rain was falling again. But it didn't wash the blood off.

Jake dropped to his knees on the dark, wet sidewalk.

After a moment he stood up.

"You weren't really there," said a soothing voice.

Jake sat up on the white cot, tugged off the Tek headgear. He didn't say anything to Dr. Weatherford.

"I want you to go back again now," she said. "This time realize that you were nowhere near Berlin when Beth Kittridge was murdered."

The Tek session had taken him to Berlin, convinced his brain that he was an on-the-spot witness to events he'd only seen on a vidwall newscast.

But it had done something else, something no one at The Institute had anticipated.

He had his memory back. He remembered now what had happened to him down in the NecroPlex. Jake also knew what he was supposed to be doing.

Leaning, he deposited the Brainbox on the floor. "I think maybe one session is enough for tonight, Doctor," he said quietly.

She studied his face for a moment. "Perhaps you're right, Jake," she said finally. "We'll wait until tomorrow night to try Tek therapy again."

"Thanks," he said. But he knew damned well he wouldn't still be here by tomorrow night.

$\equiv$27$\equiv$

THE LARGE SWIMMING pool was real, as was the shimmering blue water in it. The palm trees and the flowering shrubs surrounding it were all holographic projections. The bright sunlight also wasn't real.

Marriner, wearing a three-piece white suit, was sitting in a slingchair beside the shallow end of the pool. "I'm wondering, Lana, if I made the right decision about Jake Cardigan."

Lana Chen was a chubby Chinese woman. Wrapped in a large flowered plyotowel, she was sprawled in a lounge chair a few feet from him. "Should've killed him," she said in a lazy murmur.

"No, that wouldn't be smart," he said. "I don't want to annoy Walt Bascom and the whole damned Cosmos Detective Agency."

"You exaggerate their astuteness and their abilities," she told him, sitting up and rearranging the towel. "They'd never associate you with his death."

"What I'm talking about is planting the guy at The Institute," he said. "There were other options that might—"

"I didn't come up here to this rinky-dink satellite to talk strategy with you," said Lana. "I'm a technician and, really, interested only in getting ready for the TekNet demonstration day after tomorrow."

"Then why are you lolling around out here?"

"There's a time to work and a time to relax," she explained.

"You damn well better be ready when Anzelmo and those other Teklords arrive Tuesday."

"I'm just about set now," she assured him. "They'll all be impressed."

He rubbed his lean black hands together. "We'll be able to grab at least forty percent of the entire Tek trade with this, Lana," he said quietly.

"And you'll tick off just about every Tek cartel in the world."

He shrugged. "That doesn't bother me."

"Yet you're afraid of Bascom and the Cosmos Agency?"

"We're talking about somebody with tremendous influence on the one hand and the threat of physical violence on the other," he told the technician. "I trust my security setup, but with Bascom you never know if—"

"A moment of your time, boss." Miles/26 had come trotting out of the villa and into the bright sun of the satellite's endless noon.

Marriner left his chair, frowning, moving toward the chrome robot. "What?"

"I keep tabs, as you know, on everybody who visits the Movie Palace—tourists, tradesmen, the lot."

Marriner eyed him. "Somebody suspicious show up today?"

The robot's chrome-plated head flashed sunlight as he nodded. "A young lady checked into the Hotel Cyrano a little over an hour ago," he reported. "Her name is Natalie Dent and she's a reporter with Newz, Inc."

"I don't think I know her. Is she dangerous for some reason?"

Miles said, "Her cover story is that she's here to do a travel report for the vidwall. But Miss Dent is one of Newz' crackerjack investigative reporters."

"She can't know anything about our meeting with Anzelmo," Marriner assured him.

"She knows about something," said the robot. "And—I just double-checked on this when I spotted her name—this woman's a very close pal of Sid Gomez. And Gomez is, in turn, the—"

"Partner of Jake Cardigan." Marriner sat down again. "All right, Miles, put a watch on her."

"They've used Natalie Dent and Newz in the past to break a story and put pressure on somebody," added Miles/ 26.

"We know where Cardigan is at the moment," the black man said. "Better get me a fix on Gomez' whereabouts."

"Already working on that, boss." The robot's chrome head made a faint clanging noise when he gave his employer a lazy salute. He turned away, heading back to the villa.

Johnny Trocadero stared up at the ceiling of the nightclub. "How about that?" he remarked.

A gentle artificial snow was falling down from above. It spotted the jungle foliage of the main room with freckles of white, and dropped snowflakes on the small man's platinum hair.

"It doesn't," Yedra Cortez pointed out, "snow in the frigging jungle, midget."

"Not usually, no," the Teklord admitted. "Still and all, you know, it's an interesting effect."

"In the wrong place."

"I'll tell my technical people about it," Trocadero promised as he walked over to a table and sat down. "How's Quadrill doing?"

She, unhappy, brushed snow off her crew-cut head. "Can't you turn the damn thing off?"

"It's only snow." He beckoned to her, nodding at the chair opposite him.

Very reluctantly, Yedra went over and took the seat. "I don't like that asshole."

"Quadrill?"

"He's the asshole we're talking about, isn't he?"

"Nobody likes him," Trocadero told her.

"I'd feel a hell of a lot better if we weren't using him."

Looking up at the ceiling again, the Teklord said, "Nobody much likes the guy, but he's efficient. He took care of the Hotel Santa Clara, remember?"

"But Gomez got away."

"We didn't hire him to kill that Cosmos op," the small man reminded her. "He was supposed to take care of Glendenny."

"They found Jill Bernardino anyway."

He spread his little hands wide. "That's fate, Yedra, not some fault of Quadrill's," he said. "Don't worry, he'll remove Marriner and Anzelmo and the rest of them."

"I want some backup on this," she said, wiping snow off her bosom. "In case fate slips it to us again and Quadrill fails."

"Up to you," said Trocadero. "But let me know what you decide to do."

"Maybe," she said.

Smiling, Trocadero reached across and took hold of her

hand. "Maybe doesn't work with me," he said.

She yanked her hand free. "I'm getting damned tired of—Shit."

The snow had turned to rain.

Trocadero stood up. "We better," he suggested, "get outside where it's not raining."

The young woman rose to follow him. But instead she stopped dead, brought her hand up to her temple, grimaced. "Jesus," she murmured.

Trocadero turned, came back to her side. "What the heck's wrong?"

Gritting her teeth, Yedra bent at the middle, fisted her hands, groaned in pain.

He put an arm around her shoulders. "Hey, what is it?"

After a moment, she straightened up and jerked away from the little Teklord. "I don't know. Some sort of head-ache I guess," she said in a choked voice. "Gone now."

"It's that s-mail dingus you got planted in your sconce."

"No, the skull-mail implant is guaranteed not to cause any pain whatsoever." She looked up, briefly, into the fall-ing rain. "It's probably an allergic reaction to this stupid artificial weather contraption. Let's get out of here, huh?"

"You sure you're okay?"

"I'm fine. Forget about it." She went running through the simulated jungle toward the nearest doorway.

—═28═—

Bascom said, "Nothing. Not a thing."

"Not even from Gomez?" asked Dan.

On the phonescreen the chief of the Cosmos Detective Agency shook his head. "Sid hasn't reported in for several hours."

Dan took a step back from the deck phone. "We haven't been able to find out anything about what's happened to my dad either," he admitted forlornly.

"Be of good cheer," advised Bascom. "I'll get back to you soon as I hear anything."

Signing off, Dan walked across the deck to join Molly at the railing. The day was fading, the Pacific was darkening.

"No news, huh?"

"Nothing beyond what we already know, nope."

"It'll be okay." She took his hand.

"I keep feeling that there ought to be something else I can do to—"

A silver landcycle was coming, loudly, along the beach. It roared to a stop a few yards from the deck and a lean

Chinese in a long flapping overcoat hopped clear of the rear seat. "See you in twenty-nine minutes and eighteen seconds, kid."

The young woman in the driveseat gave him a casual wave and then sped off into the gathering dusk.

"This is the Cardigan residence, isn't it?" inquired Timecheck as he came trudging through the sand toward them.

"Sure, but my father isn't—"

"I know Jake's not here." He rolled up his coat sleeve to consult the array of watch dials built into his metal arm. "I've got an appointment with another client in twenty-eight minutes and thirteen seconds, Daniel, so what say we get down to—"

"You must be Timecheck," realized Dan. "My dad has told me about—"

"I'm world-renowned as an informant and tipster," admitted the Chinese. "The point is—Oh, good evening, Miss Fine. Excuse me for seeming to ignore you." He consulted his watches again. "Twenty-seven minutes and nine seconds to go."

"Do you know something about where my father is?"

Timecheck gave an affirmative nod. "Yes, and I've been trying to contact Gomez to pass the information along, but he's not returning my calls," he explained. "Bascom's not too kindly disposed toward me. So I decided to come to you. Three hundred dollars."

"You're trying to *sell* us information?" asked Molly.

The informant climbed up onto the deck. "That's my profession, remember?"

"Seems to me," she said, "if you're such a good friend of Jake Cardigan's, that you wouldn't—"

"Jake's a pal *and* a customer," he amplified.

Dan said, "That's all right, Molly. We'll pay you, Timecheck. You may, though, have to wait until—"

"I trust you, Dan." He held out his flesh hand and they shook. Timecheck boosted himself up onto the railing and sat with his back to the twilight ocean.

"Well?" said Dan.

"In the course of digging up some information for your father," he began, pausing to consult his arm, "I came across something about his current whereabouts."

"You know where he is?"

Timecheck replied, "Let us say, rather, that I know where Jake is supposed to be."

The skinny red-haired girl shook her head. "Naw, I don't need a damn thing, greaser," she assured Gomez.

They were standing beside his skycar and the day was ending all around them. "You helped me get clear of those goons, *chiquita*, and—"

"Hey, I was saving my ass as well as yours."

Gomez nodded. "Maybe you'd like to shake the Tek habit and—"

"You're not cut out to be a preacher." Snooky laughed.

"*Sí*, but it's a shame to see you tangled up with—"

"My life, not yours."

"*Es verdad*." Gomez reached out, put a hand on her thin shoulder. "My name's Sid Gomez and I work for the Cosmos Detective Agency. If you ever need any—"

"You really think, Gomez, that I'd turn to a private cop for help?"

"Someday, sometime. It's possible." Smiling, he climbed into his skycar.

The girl smiled back, then went hurrying off into the new night.

• • •

The cambot said, "That makes three, Nat."

Natalie Dent paused in the center of the living room carpet of her suite in the Hotel Cyrano. She dropped the hand holding the small bug-detector to her side, wrinkled her freckled nose and told the robot, "Although I'm noted for being an exceptionally calm and even-tempered person, Sidebar, even when working on some horrendously dangerous assignments for Newz, Inc., I must mention that I get a mite annoyed when you address me as Nat. My name—the name, I might add, by which billions of loyal vidwall viewers know and respect me as one of the top investigative reporters on, or off, the planet—is Natalie. Not Nat, a nick-name that only vulgar rowdies and hooligans and that disreputable and quick-tongued private eye Sid Gomez address me by."

"Maybe," suggested the robot from the sofa where he was sitting and gazing out at the sunny private patio, "you ought to keep your lip buttoned, Natalie, until you locate and disarm *all* the listening and viewing devices that have been planted in our suite."

The auburn-haired vidwall reporter said, "Far be it from me to complain about doing my fair share of the work. However, if you'd lend a hand instead of merely reclining there on your rusty wusty, Sidebar, then the task would be completed a heck of a lot—"

"Rusty dusty," the camera robot corrected, turning both his head and the lens mounted in his metallic chest in her direction.

She began pacing the room again, swinging the detecting device, slowly, from side to side. "It doesn't seem especially apt," said Natalie, "for a mechanism to be questioning the proper usage of a—Oops."

The small gadget in her hand had commenced blinking the tiny bead of red light on its topside.

Natalie knelt on a stretch of carpeting near the arched doorway to her bedroom. She moved the detector over the surface of the carpet. "There it is, an extremely teeny one." The gadget had plucked a very small audiovisual bug from the pile.

"Four so far," observed Sidebar.

It took Natalie, working unaided, another hour and a half to sweep the entire suite. "I'm wondering," she said as she returned to the living room, "why anyone would go to the trouble of installing nine spying devices in my quarters." She sat on the edge of an armchair, jingling the bugs on her palm. "I don't imagine that every suite in this establishment is this profusely packed with eavesdropping gear."

"It might just be," suggested the camera robot, "that somebody hereabouts suspects the real reason we've come up to the Movie Palace."

—=29=—

GOMEZ DIRECTED HIS skycar eastward into the night. Hunching slightly in his seat, he punched out a number on the dash vidphone.

An answering robot appeared on the screen. "Cosmos Detective Agency, office of Walt Bascom. Who shall I say is—Oh, it's you, Gomez. Where the dickens have you been?"

"Otherwise occupied. Is the *jefe*—"

"We've been trying to contact you."

"What's afoot?"

"I'll let him tell you."

The screen displayed the Cosmos logo for ten seconds and then Bascom, scowling, appeared.

"We have a lead on Jake's possible location, Sid. Dan Cardigan just came here to pass it along to me," said Bascom. "What have you been up to?"

Gomez replied, "I've been finding out where they shipped Jake."

Dan moved into view behind the agency chief. "Does this involve Doc Sears?"

179

"Buenas noches," he said to Jake's son. "How'd you find out about Sears?"

"Timecheck stopped by the condo. Said he couldn't get in touch with you, so he—"

"I was concentrating on saving my butt and then tracking down Doc Sears."

"Have you found him yet? We were just about to start a—"

"Doc is rumored to be gone to ground somewhere in the vastness of Mexico."

"But you do know where my father is?"

"Your *padre* is, almost certainly, being held at a private facility calling itself The Institute. It's located—"

"Near the New Haven Enclave in Connecticut," supplied Bascom, still scowling. "It's supposed to be a legit psych center for very rich nutcases. But they've been known to help certain influential customers keep people out of circulation."

"*Sí,* and that's—"

"Is that where Dad is?" asked Dan. "How can you be sure, if you couldn't find Doc Sears?"

"I was able," answered Gomez as his skycar sped east, "to contact the gent who assisted the elusive Doc Sears in processing Jake after those Limey louts turned him over."

"What did they do to him?"

"A simple mindwipe—it was a rush job—and then they planted some false memories," said Gomez. "Nothing too serious, nothing that can't be reversed."

"What's their game?" asked Bascom. "Why dump Jake back there?"

"According to the information I was able to persuade this *pendejo* to pass along, the Anzelmo/Marriner combo wants to keep Jake out of the way for a week or so."

Bascom nodded. "Until after they have their secret meeting."

"That's the idea, *sí.*"

"You're on your way to Connecticut?"

"Even as we speak."

"I can arrange to have some ops there to back you up
when—"

"No, *por favor.* I think I'll do better more or less on my
own."

The agency head said, "Okay, Sid. But contact me if
anything comes up that—"

"You're certain he's alive?" cut in Dan.

"Jake's alive," Gomez assured him, "and he's going to
continue in that condition."

It was windy in Connecticut.

A harsh, strong wind blew across the gravel path that
went twisting up to the porch of the rustic cabin that the
long, lean man with the double-barreled lazrifle was leading
Gomez toward.

"Here you are, Mr. Gomez." The caretaker halted.

"*Gracias.*" Gomez went double-timing up the realwood
steps.

The door of the cabin opened inward. "C'mon in, Sid,"
invited the woman who stood there. "I've been doing some
nosing around since I got your call." She was just over
four feet tall and her left shoe was built up.

Bowing, the detective took her hand, bent lower to kiss
it. "Good to see you again, Maggie."

"Sure, I imagine I'm a pleasant relief after all your beautiful ex-wives." Limping, Maggie Pennoyer crossed her
living room. "At least, I give you a lot less trouble."

"Actually, *cara,* only two of the set have given me excessive trouble."

"I don't think you'll ever be interested in a normal everyday woman who didn't heap grief on you," suggested Maggie. "Not that I'm anywhere near being a normal everyday woman myself."

Gomez said, "I got in touch with you, Maggie, because you're the leading freelance expert on brainwiping and on reversing its effects. And it looks like Jake is presently a reluctant resident of a joint called The Institute, which lies just over fifty miles north of your little hideaway."

"So you mentioned on the vidphone." Making a follow-me gesture, she hobbled across the rustic room to a doorway.

Gomez followed. "Dan Cardigan was a guest of yours a few months ago."

"He's a nice, decent young man," she said as they walked along the hallway. "Hard to believe he's turned out so well, considering he's got Jake for a father and a ne'er-do-well lothario like you as an honorary uncle."

"*Chiquita*, I'm so virtuous all sorts of high-ranking clerics come to me to ask advice on how to be more pious," he assured her. "Despite your lack of perception when it comes to a fellow's character, you did a good job of untangling the damage those louts had tried to do his mind."

"Hey, that's what I'm dedicated to," she reminded. "Undoing the work of all the doinks—government loons and criminal schmucks—who try to use mind bending as one of the tools of their trade."

In a small room off the hall Maggie had one of her offices. Next to the realwood desk stood a small, low holostage. On it now was a cutaway projection of a sprawling building.

She limped over to the stage, pointing. "This is a simulation, in perfect scale, of the wing of The Institute where they're holding Jake.''

''*Bueno*. Then he is definitely there?''

''Yep, sure. I have a connection at that dump and I confirmed it right after you phoned me from the Coast.''

Bending his knees, Gomez took a closer look at the projection. ''That's Jake's room there—where the little red dot of light is blinking?''

''That's it.'' Maggie used her finger as a pointer. ''Now, Sid, you ought to be able to get in by way of this entrance here. It's where supplies for this poor man's Bedlam are delivered.''

''Your contact can arrange that?''

''My contact and me. I'll fix it so you can hitch a ride on a produce skyvan that's due to—'' Her wristphone had started to pulse. ''Hold on a sec.''

He noticed that when Maggie pressed the answer button, the tiny screen remained blank.

''News for you,'' announced a blurred voice.

''About him?''

''Not there anymore.''

''Where'd he go?''

''Not sure. But was sprung from room.''

''Who took him?''

''Not sure.''

''Any idea where?''

''Probably into the Wilderness Preserve.''

''Thanks.'' Maggie ended the call and let her arm swing down to her side.

''I take it,'' said Gomez, ''that your conversation pertains to Jake.''

Maggie nodded, frowning. ''Hell and damnation,'' she observed. ''Who the devil broke him out of there?''

"Maybe he escaped on his own."

"Doubtful."

"Okay, and what's this Wilderness Preserve your chum mentioned?"

"It can be a damn dangerous place," answered Maggie.

—≡30≡—

ANDREW SIMMONDS SIGHED out a breath. He slowed, then stopped still on the forest path they were following. "Damn leg's bothering me," he explained to Jake as he leaned, crouched and took a slap at what appeared to be a fallen log.

When his hand went through the projection, Jake told him, "If you're looking for something to sit on, that big grey rock yonder is real."

The former OCO agent straightened up. "You can tell from here?"

"I'm good at differentiating the real from the fake."

"The trouble with this Wilderness Preserve, too much of it is holographic or simulated." Simmonds prodded the rock with his forefinger. "Real sure enough. You were right, Cardigan." He seated himself.

Jake glanced back the way they'd come. "We're about five miles from The Institute," he said, "with no sign of pursuit yet. But still, I'd like to keep moving."

Carefully, the older man rolled up his trouser leg. "I'll be okay in a couple minutes more," he assured Jake, rubbing at the metallic leg. "This thing gives me a lot of pain some nights."

"You can sit here till morning, Simmonds. But I want to—"

"I helped you break out of that place," reminded Simmonds. "You ought not to abandon me in the wilds."

"This is a preserve, not the forest primeval."

"Besides," the other man added, "we had a deal. I get you clear of The Institute and you put in a good word for me with Bascom. See if he—"

"That escape you arranged," put in Jake, "went very smoothly."

"So? I'm good at this sort of thing."

"But you never tried it until I was dumped here."

Simmonds said, "Well, Cardigan, I guess it's time to admit that I haven't been completely truthful with you."

"Who're you working for?"

The former government agent spread his hands wide. "Not the Office of Clandestine Operations," he insisted. "No, I'm doing what you might call freelance work now."

"Who for?" Jake eased closer to the seated man. The fallen leaves underfoot made realistic crackling noises.

"Some people who are interested in talking to you," Simmonds answered. He rested his hand on the side of his silvery artificial leg. "I was never actually a patient in there. I simply bribed my way in and out."

"What a surprise," said Jake quietly. "You haven't identified your employers."

"Let's just say they're some people who are interested in why Leon Marriner is collaborating with the likes of Anzelmo and his bunch."

Jake grinned. "I don't think I much want to meet these folks."

"You don't have any choice, Cardigan." Simmonds

moved his hand a few inches lower on his metal leg. "Because I'm going to deliver you to them. In fact—"

"Nope." Jake dived forward just as the one-time OCO man clicked open a panel in the chrome leg.

Inside the panel rested a small stungun. Simmonds clutched it and started to tug it out.

But Jake straightened up, took a step back and kicked out.

His booted foot caught the seated man square on the chin.

Gasping, head jerking back, Simmonds was lifted up. He half turned, swayed, fell to his left.

Jake followed him, grabbing the hand that was clutching the gun.

Simmonds cried out in pain and dropped the weapon.

Jake hit him twice, hard, in the stomach.

The other man stumbled, fell back against the trunk of an oak tree. This was a real tree and his head hit it. He groaned, sighed, fell toward a clump of brush.

The brush was holographic and he dropped into it and was surrounded by green.

Scooping up the stungun, Jake glanced around.

He pointed the gun at the sprawled Simmonds and fired. "That'll keep you unconscious for a few hours," he said.

Tucking the weapon into a pocket, Jake knelt beside the fallen man. He searched him, his clothes and the other compartments in the metal leg. He didn't find anything he could use—no other weapons, no palmphone and nothing about who might've hired him to deliver Jake to them.

A moment later he was moving along the dark night trail.

There were dark trees and deep shadows all around Jake as he traveled through the forest.

He figured he had to get clear of the Wilderness Preserve by dawn.

Then he'd head for someplace where he could contact Gomez or Bascom.

The folks who'd had him brainwiped and dumped in storage at The Institute hadn't done a very efficient job.

Most of his memory was coming back to him.

Jake wondered who'd sent Simmonds to break him out.

''Got to be careful,'' he warned himself.

The erstwhile Office of Clandestine Operations agent had been intending to turn Jake over to his employers.

Which meant he'd probably arranged a rendezvous spot here in this simulated wilderness.

Jake didn't want to run into the people sent to pick him up.

Off to his right now he became aware of the faint sound of movement.

It sounded as though something, or someone, was moving through the dark woodlands parallel to the path Jake was following.

Eyes narrowed, he scanned the forest as he kept striding along the trail.

He didn't see anything.

He covered another quarter of a mile, listening carefully.

There was still something following along beside him to his right.

Jake eased off the trail, stepping around a real maple tree on his left. He pushed farther into the woodlands, making his way around authentic oaks and maples and right through projected pines.

He kept going in the direction that the trail was heading, hunched and watchful.

Then he heard a faint crackling noise behind him.

Before he could turn, the barrel of a gun was poked into his back.

"Stop right there, Cardigan," suggested a thin nasal voice.

$=31=$

HIGH UP IN the bright sunny midday sky a seagull produced a sudden strange bonging noise. Its wings folded in at its sides and it came plummeting down to land a few feet from Natalie Dent on the simulated yellow sand of Surf Beach.

"Shoddy workmanship," commented Sidebar, aiming his built-in vidcam down at the fallen mechanical bird.

"Concentrate on the people out there frolicking in the fake ocean," urged the reporter. "We don't want to give the impression that we're up here in the Movie Palace satellite preparing some sort of muckraking documentary."

Ignoring her, the robot cameraman booted the gull with his metal foot. "Muckrakers don't waste their time on sweatshop bots," he pointed out.

"Nevertheless, I've been feeling extremely uneasy ever since I discovered, with absolutely no help from you, Sidebar, those very sophisticated eavesdropping devices in my suite," she told him, taking hold of his metal elbow and tugging him along the imitation beach. "What impressed me the most, and keep in mind that I'm noted for not going to pieces under pressure, was the quantity of the darn bugs.

They must be deeply suspicious of me if they went through the trouble of concealing a whole stewpot of the things heather and yon in—''

"Hither," corrected the robot.

"You may not remember this, Sidebar, but only last year I won a Congeniality Award from the Vidwall Reporters of the World Association," said Natalie. "So, when I criticize you, as I feel obliged to do now, it isn't because I'm a habitual nag or have an inflated opinion of my worth. No, it's because I really think you're becoming increasingly uppity, and all these corrections of my vocabulary and use of the language are really not contributing to my morale."

"A tin cup with your name scratched on it doesn't make you a pillar of virtue, Nat."

Natalie concentrated on her breathing for a silent moment. Then she pointed at the very believable waves that were coming in from the imitation stretch of ocean. "Get me some footage of that big handsome chap on the surfboard."

"Lad with the blue hair?"

She nodded, walking a few steps away from him and digging her bare toes into the sand. "He seems to be the most innocuous person hereabouts and that should convince them we're on a completely innocent mission."

As his camera whirred, Sidebar said, "It's probable, Nat, that Marriner and his crew have already tumbled onto your real purpose. In which case, our wisest course would be to scram."

"Natalie Dent never scrams," she told the bot. "Courage runs in the Dent family and . . . What is it?"

The robot had brought a metal hand up to his chest, pressing it to the lens of the camera. "I'm feeling . . . feeling . . ."

Sidebar's left leg gave way under him. He sagged, sat down hard on the yellow beach.

Natalie ran back to his side and reached down toward him.

He came falling sideways, the weight of his torso brushing her hand aside. The robot dropped down on the imitation sand and ceased to function.

"Sidebar, you just had a tune-up," she said, kneeling beside the sprawled mechanical man.

"How unfortunate." Someone put a hand on the young woman's shoulder. "You and your stricken robot better come along with us, Miss Dent."

Turning to face the heavyset black man, Jake inquired, "Who you working for?"

"An organization you don't want to mess with, Cardigan," he responded, moving the hand that held the gun a few inches from side to side.

"You're not from The Institute, come to fetch me back?"

"Those jerks, no." He shook his head.

"Then you must be with the gang Simmonds was planning to deliver me to."

"I'm with a gang, Cardigan, that you damn well better start showing some respect for," he told him. "Using a stunner on Simmonds isn't going to make anybody too happy—and you'll regret it."

Grinning, Jake said, "I'm awed and impressed. How many of your cohorts are in the woods here with you?"

"You've been a gumshoe too long," suggested the black man. "It makes you way too inquisitive." He gestured with the gun. "Now get your ass back on the trail."

"Here's another inquiry. Where are we heading?"

"To meet my cohorts. Move."

Jake shrugged and took a few steps in the direction of the pathway.

The man with the gun suddenly grunted in pain.

Stumbling over nothing, he sank to his knees and then went toppling over into a patch of real moss.

Jake lunged to grab up the fallen stungun.

"Leave it lay, mister." A thin boy, not more than eleven from the look of him, stepped into view. He held a stunrifle aimed at Jake.

—= 32 =—

TWO MORE RAGGED boys came drifting out of the dark woods. The one who was taller and about fifteen carried a lazrifle and the other, thin and not more than thirteen, clutched a stungun in his skinny left hand.

"Stand back some, mister," suggested the eleven-year-old who held his stunrifle aimed at Jake's middle.

"Who are you lads?" he asked them.

The oldest boy squatted beside the unconscious man and commenced searching him. "Some Banx chits," he answered as he pulled a wad of the yellow money chits from one coat pocket.

"He had that stungun too, Rufe," mentioned the boy who was guarding Jake.

Rufe continued with his searching of the sprawled man. "Take it, Tunney."

The thirteen-year-old bent and caught up the fallen weapon. "Got it."

Jake grinned. "Bandits. That what you guys are?"

Rufe said, "Search him too, Tunney."

The thin boy approached Jake and poked the stungun in

his side. "You escape from the bin back there?"

"Yeah."

"Shit," he complained as he began searching. "That means that soon as they notice you're missing, they'll come hunting."

"You live in the preserve?"

"Naw, in one of the Welfare Compounds over near the Bridgeport Redoubt."

"We come over here once in a while to prowl around," explained the boy with the rifle. "Sometimes we run into somebody who's wandering around like you and that other guy. But mainly it's because there are lots of animals roaming the woods. You know, you can sell them in the compounds."

"Poachers," said Jake. "Have you run into anybody else hereabouts tonight?"

"Three assholes over near the main control station." Rufe stood up and away from the black man. "Part of this doink's crew I'd guess. They looking for you?"

"Apparently so, yeah."

"Why?"

"He was about to explain that when oblivion caught up with him."

"They cops?"

"No, more likely either government agents or just plain mercenaries."

"You important then?"

"To them," answered Jake. "How far from here did you spot this trio?"

"Couple miles at most."

Tunney made a disgusted noise and moved back from him, holding the borrowed stungun in his hand. "He's got nothing on him but this," he reported to Rufe.

"Sure, they must've taken all his stuff away from him back at The Institute."

"That they did," confirmed Jake.

Rufe said, "We better decide what to—Christ."

The trees had started to vanish, shimmering for a few seconds before they were gone. Everything that was a holographic projection went away at once.

They were now in the middle of a wide field that contained only two oak trees and a few scatterings of low real scrub.

Then the ground started to glow. Litepanels that had been hidden by the pastoral projections came to life and an intense yellow brightness rose up and went spreading across acre after acre of blank ground.

"Jesus," said Tunney, "they're going to come hunting you, mister."

"They turned off the wilderness," added Rufe. He thrust the things he'd taken from the unconscious man into a tattered pocket, spun and started running from there.

The other two boys followed, losing all interest in Jake.

Bascom, legs dangling, was sitting on the edge of his desk in his tower office. He was playing a twentieth-century bebop tune, "Un Poco Loco," on his sax.

The vidphone atop his desk spoke. "Important call."

"Pertaining to what?"

"A large fee. And possibly the case Gomez and Cardigan are engaged with."

"Who's calling?"

"Madeline McHambrick of Newz, Inc."

"We'll talk." Abandoning his saxophone and dropping to the floor, the chief of the Cosmos Detective Agency went scooting around to settle into his desk chair.

Madeline McHambrick was a blonde woman in her forties. "Sorry to bother you at this hour, Bascom, but—"

"We never sleep," he assured her. "You're the associate CEO at Newz, Inc., are you not?"

"Hell, I run the whole damn shebang. In spite of what our half-assed publicity staff says."

Bascom asked, "Why do you want to hire Cosmos?"

She said, "I've heard you're something of a scoundrel."

"Not something of, I am a dyed-in-the-wool, certified one hundred percent scoundrel."

"Good. That's what we need," said McHambrick. "You know Natalie Dent, don't you?"

"Not well. She is, however, the dear and revered chum of one of my most admirable operatives, Sid Gomez, and he—"

"Spare me the bullshit, Bascom. I know all about Gomez," cut in the Newz executive. "Now, here's what I want you to do."

"Proceed."

"Natalie, along with that odious cambot of hers, has disappeared."

"Give me some details," he requested.

"I assume you won't go blabbing any of this to our vidwall news rivals."

"Not unless they offer me more money then you're going to pay us."

She told him, "Natalie had a tip, from one of her most reliable informants, that an important meeting between certain important European Teklords and a very influential electronics tycoon was going to take place on—"

"Anzelmo and Marriner."

McHambrick blinked. "You know about that?"

"Pretty much, sure."

"Then you also know that Marriner and those Tek thugs

are meeting tomorrow evening up in the Movie Palace satellite?''

"Knew that, yes,'' lied Bascom.

"Well, we shipped Natalie and her camera robot up there yesterday. Her cover was that she was simply doing a travel report on the Movie Palace,'' continued the blonde woman. "But when one of our producers tried to phone Natalie today, she was told that Natalie wasn't there. Wasn't registered at any of the hotels, had never arrived.''

"How come you just don't send more of your own people up there to hunt around for her?''

"I don't want to risk losing any more of my staff, Bascom.''

The agency head smiled. "We'll accept the assignment.''

"What's the fee?''

He told her.

She said, "That's outrageous.''

"It does border on the outrageous,'' he agreed. "But, according to you, my operatives will probably be risking death up there.''

"All right, very well,'' she said. "I accept your onerous terms.''

"We'll vidfax you a contract,'' he promised. "I'll put some of my best ops on it at once.''

"Will one of them be that rascal Gomez?''

"It just,'' answered Bascom, "might be.''

Flying at an altitude of 10,000 feet, Gomez was leaning back in the driveseat of his skycar and, with tongue pressed to the back of his teeth, whistling faintly.

The voxbox below the scanner screen mounted on the dash said, "We're approaching the Wilderness Preserve in question.''

An image blossomed on the small rectangular screen.

"*Qué pasa*? What's going on down there?" inquired the detective.

The screen showed flat empty fields that held only a few trees and were glaringly illuminated from below.

"They've shut down all the holographic projections," said the voxbox.

Gomez touched the controls and the skycar began descending. "Find me some human beings down below," he requested of the scanner.

"Three raggedy boys, running like blazes," said the voxbox.

He glanced at the screen. "I'm looking for somebody more closely resembling Jake."

"Think we got him."

Jake, crouched low and surrounded by light, appeared on the screen.

"*Sí*, that's him," said Gomez, smiling. "Let's come to earth on that spot."

"Landing pattern arranged," said the voxbox after a few seconds.

As the skycar dropped down through the night, Gomez kept his eyes on the screen most of the time.

"Here's something else you ought to take notice of." The screen showed him two men, armed with lazrifles, moving rapidly along a path between fields of light.

"How far from Jake?"

"Half a mile."

Gomez touched a key on the control pad and the speed of the descending car increased. "We have to get to him *muy pronto*."

—≡ 33 ≡—

"I SUPPOSE COMPLAINING about the accommodations in what is, for all practical purposes, a detention cell is somewhat on the ludicrous side," Natalie Dent was saying in the direction of the spread-eagled camera robot. "Still and all, this is an awfully tacky room they've dumped us into and there isn't even a window, let alone a view. You'd expect that a satellite that boasts of being both a posh resort and a first-rate production facility would toss even abject prisoners into better quarters than this."

She jiggled a few times in the metallic chair she'd been tied to with plazrope.

Sprawled on the stained carpeting, Sidebar now made a ratcheting, groaning noise. "Where am I?" he asked, eyes clicking open.

"Flat on your back in a shabby hotel room."

The bot, eyes blinking rapidly, sat up. "Some phud used a disabler on me."

"Yes," the reporter confirmed. "Then a large brutish man forced me here, while two unkempt goons hauled you along."

Sidebar rubbed at his side. "Looks like they let me drag on the pavement for a while. I'm all scuffed."

"I'll have you burnished soon as we get out of this."

"Oh? And when do you plan to depart this hole, Nat?"

Giving a sad shrug, she answered, "Well, Sidebar, I'm not exactly certain."

"I warned you that we were bound to annoy Marriner. Tycoons are very touchy people."

"That well may be, but I have a very pervasive reputation around the globe—and Newz, Inc., isn't an organization even tycoons want to dare messing with."

"Not exactly so." Part of the wall had slid aside and Lana Chen stepped into the room. As she passed the seated robot on her way over to the bound reporter, the heavyset Chinese woman kicked him in the backside and said, "You can be disabled again in a flash, big boy. So maintain something approaching good behavior."

The robot rubbed again at his scratched metal side.

Natalie said, "Just who might you be, miss, and why in the world have I been treated so badly? Freedom of the press is, after all, a basic right that is guaranteed by—"

"If you'll, please, shut the hell up for a moment, Miss Dent," said Lana, "I'll be able to explain to you what's going on."

"I'm fully aware of what's going on. I've been abducted in broad daylight—well, I suppose that's redundant, since it's always broad daylight up here in the Movie Palace. Let's simply say that I have been kidnapped against my will and shoved in this dismal—"

"Quiet, please." Lana made her right hand into a fist and hit Natalie in the upper arm, hard. "Listen to me. That's all you have to do, Miss Dent. We don't require, at the moment, any commentary."

"Physical abuse just adds to the offense."

Lana hit her again and leaned closer. "What we want to know is what prompted you to come nosing around up here at the Movie Palace."

"That's quite simple," answered Natalie. "In fact, your publicity office already has a fully executed request for permission to do a travel report on—"

"Who told you about the meeting?" Lana put her face even nearer to the reporter's.

"What meeting?"

"The meeting, dear, that you're here to spy on."

Natalie cleared her throat. "You obviously have very little notion as to what sort of code reporters operate under," she said. "I can't possibly reveal my sources to you or anyone. I simply will not do that."

Lana stepped back and smiled. "Oh, you will. Trust me, you really will."

Looking up, Jake recognized the skycar that was speeding down through the night in his direction.

The flying vehicle leveled off a few feet above the bright-lit ground and hovered. "Hop aboard, *amigo*," invited Gomez.

The door on the passenger side popped open and swung out.

Sprinting, Jake ran for it.

"Not yet, Cardigan." A big man carrying a lazgun was trotting across the flat glaring field on the right.

Paying him no mind, Jake jumped for the skycar.

He landed in the cabin and the door snapped shut just as the beam of the lazgun went crackling across the space Jake had been occupying outside.

"Who's that *cabrón*?" inquired his partner.

The skycar rose rapidly up.

Jake answered, "I'm not certain. He's probably affiliated

with a onetime OCO agent named Simmonds.''

Gomez turned the skycar to the south. "Would that be Andrew Simmonds?''

"Yep. Know him?''

"He works for, last time I heard—''

"Hold on a minute, Sid. Something I want to check on.'' Toward the dash scanner Jake said, "Seen three kids down there anyplace?''

"Spotted them a few minutes back. Hold on—Yeah, here they are again.''

The screen showed the three ragged boys running. The smallest tripped, fell, landed flat out. Rufe stopped, came back and helped him up.

"Like to give them a lift out of here,'' said Jake. "If nobody minds?''

"*Sí*, we can do that,'' agreed his partner.

The skycar started to drop down again.

"Who are these three *niños*?''

"Poachers who tried to hold me up.''

"Oh so?''

"Don't want to see them picked up by Simmonds' cronies or any goons from The Institute.''

Gomez nodded. "As for the defrocked OCO agent—my sources say he is now employed by a DC outfit that calls itself the Friends of Electronic Research.''

"Lobbyists?''

"Among other things,'' answered Gomez. "They're a bit more active than that in the political life of our great nation.''

"And they might be interested in what Marriner is up to?''

"The dues-paying members are all rivals of that bright lad.''

"Ragamuffins directly below,'' announced the voxbox.

"Set us down a few yards ahead of them," instructed Jake.

When the skycar was hovering directly in the running boys' path, Jake leaned out the open door and called, "Care for a lift, fellas?"

"Screw you," said Tunney. "You'll turn us over to the law."

"Nope, you have my word," Jake assured him. "C'mon. We want to get clear of here."

Rufe said, "Okay, we accept. But no lectures, no sermons."

"Not even a request for an apology," Jake promised.

Rufe nodded and the three of them came scrambling aboard.

— 34 —

YOU COULD SEE the flames and the black smoke spiraling up into the greying night sky from a long way off.

Rufe said, "Better land on the outskirts of our Welfare Compound."

"What's that burning?" inquired Gomez, guiding the skycar groundward.

"Nothing special," answered Tunney, who was hunched near a window at the rear of the compartment. "We have lots of fires down there."

"No use," said Rufe, "you getting too close."

It was an apartment building, one which looked to be over a century old, that was burning in the coming dawn.

"Can you guys get back into the compound okay?" asked Jake as the car landed in a weedy lot a good half-mile from the high neowood fence surrounding the compound.

The skycar bounced twice, swerved slightly to the left. "Oops," remarked Gomez. "I think I hit something."

"Just a dead dog," said Tunney. "Nothing to worry about."

When the door on the passenger side flapped open, the mingled smells of burning, decay and offal came rushing inside.

Jake passed Rufe a handful of Banx chits. "Thanks for taking care of that lout who was trying to waylay me."

"We would've taken care of you too, probably, if they hadn't shut down the forest and come hunting." Rufe took the money and dropped clear of the skycar.

The other two boys, saying nothing, followed him.

"Adiós, muchachos," called Gomez.

The door shut, the skycar climbed up into the beginning day.

"Have you noticed," asked Jake, "that there are still several problems of our society that don't seem to have gotten solved?"

"Sí, that very thought occurred to me the last time I went slumming," replied his partner.

The voxbox under the phonescreen said, "It's the boss man, fellas."

"He's probably anxious to know your fate, Jake," said Gomez. "Let's have the call."

"What's your current work schedule, Sid?" asked Bascom three seconds after his lined face showed up on the screen. "What I mean is—do you only report in to me every other day? Or is it—"

"It's difficult to report promptly, *jefe,* when one is being pursued by crazed killers, social misfits, women who were ill treated in their youth and thus seek—"

"You got Jake out of that joint?"

"We collaborated on that," put in Jake, leaning toward the dash phone.

"Good," said the head of the Cosmos Detective Agency. "Get over to the Stamford Enclave there in Connecticut. Check in with our special field operative Paul Moonjohn.

He'll have your phony passport cards and he'll work on your mugs until they—''

''Whoa,'' requested Jake. ''Where are we going that we need fake IDs and new faces?''

''I wish I had time to make the smartass remark that you've just set yourself up for,'' lamented Bascom. ''However, you two are traveling up to the Movie Palace satellite. You'll leave from the Westchester spaceport in—let's see— three hours and forty-seven minutes.''

''Marriner owns that satellite,'' said Jake. ''So is that where the famous get-together is taking place?''

''It is. On top of which—Sid's old ladyfriend the notorious Natalie Dent has gone missing up there and her bosses—and Lord knows why they want her back, but they do—have hired Cosmos to locate her.''

''*Dios*,'' muttered Gomez, slumping in the driveseat. ''That *mujer* is back to blight my life.''

Bascom made an impatient noise before giving them what details he'd obtained from the client and his own researchers. He concluded, ''Since Marriner and several of his people know what you gents look like—a mild disguise and a change of identification is in order.''

''Is Newz, Inc., paying an enormous fee for this caper?'' inquired Gomez.

''Not only enormous, but outrageous.''

''*Bueno*,'' said Gomez. ''Then my sacrifice in having to encounter Natalie again won't be entirely in vain.''

''You damn well better encounter her,'' said Bascom. ''And while you're up there on the Movie Palace, find out everything there is to learn about TekNet.''

''That won't give us any time to buy souvenirs,'' complained Gomez, ending the call.

•   •   •

Paul Moonjohn said, "I can't do all that much in the short amount of time you and Bascom are allowing." He was a large grey-bearded man, pale and wide.

"All we have to do, Pablo," Gomez told him, "is resemble the people on our passport cards a trifle more."

"The smartest way to have done this," complained Moonjohn, shuffling across his grey-walled little lab, "would've been to let me remodel you first. Then we take the damned triop photos."

"Bascom," reminded Jake, "works in mysterious ways."

"Okay, Sid, I'll do your face first." The big man pulled on a pair of plyogloves as he approached the chair the curly-haired detective was occupying. "That's a lousy nose whoever whipped up these passport pics stuck on you."

"*Sí*, it's nowhere near as handsome as the one I now possess."

"Only thing I can use on you is sinflesh," said Moonjohn. "It's not as convincing as some of the materials available, but because of the time factor—"

"Bascom's got us booked to catch the Movie Palace shuttle in less than three hours," reminded Jake, who was sitting in the chair next to his partner.

"Okay, fine, I'll do a rush job," said Moonjohn. "But if anybody spots that either one of you guys is a fraud—well, don't blame me."

"If somebody spots us," said Jake, "we aren't going to have time to file a complaint."

The elderly Anzelmo spat on the golden carpeting. "And they got the frapping nerve to call this the Imperial Suite?" he said in a loud, angry voice. "This shithole?"

Across the wide living room Julie was making nervous be-quiet gestures and waving the bug-detector he held in his left hand. "Mr. Anzelmo, remember what we discussed earlier about not having any conversations until—"

"Do I care who hears me?" asked the old Teklord. "I drag my weary ass from England all the way up to this goddamn Movie Palace so I can attend this hush-hush meeting and Marriner sticks me in a room that'd make a peanut feel cramped."

"It is, they assured me at the desk, the largest and most lavish suite in the entire Chateau Hollywood Hotel, sir."

"Who assured you? Some fag robot."

"I don't think robots can have sexual preferences, Mr. Anzelmo, and besides, there's no reason why Mr. Marriner would house you in a suite that's anything less than—"

"And what kind of lousy view is this?" Anzelmo went shuffling over to the wide window. "Palm trees, for Christ sake. Palm trees and a bunch of skinny broads with their little bitty asses hanging out of their swim togs."

"It's what you call a Hollywood ambiance, sir."

Pointing at the control panel next to the window, Anzelmo said, "What else can you dial up in the way of a view?"

Julie squinted. "Well, it's mostly just variations, sir. More palm trees, more starlets, more sand on the beach. Oh, and seagulls. Would you like to see a dozen more seagulls swooping in the midday sun?"

"Sheep," said Anzelmo, turning his back on the view.

"Beg pardon?"

"I want," said the Teklord evenly, "to see frigging sheep. Lots of them out in a green meadow with a bunch of cute little goddamn thatched cottages in the background."

"We don't seem to have that option, sir."

Very stiffly, the older man sat suddenly down on the

edge of a fat grey armchair. ''Well, shitcan, arrange it so that we do.''

''Don't you want me to get rid of all the eavesdropping devices first?''

''I want,'' Anzelmo repeated, ''to see sheep out the window.''

— 35 —

GOMEZ, BOTH HANDS sunk deep in his trouser pockets, was slumped in the least comfortable chair in their shuttle compartment. "This *nariz* that Moonjohn stuck on me," he complained, gingerly touching at his new nose, "will be the ruin of me."

"It's only temporary," reminded Jake. He was standing at the small circular viewindow.

"Did you notice the disdainful look our lovely blonde attendant gave me when she served our complimentary snack?"

"She's an android, Sid."

"You're insinuating I'm incapable of charming a mechanism any longer?"

"Not with that schnoz apparently."

Gomez touched it again. "This thing is sapping my self-esteem."

"You've got an ample supply," Jake assured him, "so don't fret."

"No more disguises after this. From hence, I'll risk recognition."

213

"I don't think you want Marriner's crew—or any of Anzelmo's bunch—to spot you and realize who you are."

"I suppose not." He touched the nose yet again.

"Attention," spoke the voxbox in the metal ceiling. "We will be docking next at the Movie Palace satellite. All passengers for that destination will assemble in five minutes at Exit 12–14. Repeating. We'll . . ."

Sighing, Gomez rose. "Well, let's slink to Exit 12–14." He extracted his single suitcase from the shelf. "Aren't you at all chagrined by the present stage of your own looks?"

Jake grinned. "Not particularly," he said. "In fact, I think I look splendid with grey hair. Splendid and distinguished."

"I was alluding to that extra chin."

"I have such a strong faith in my inner goodness that the state of my outward self doesn't affect me at all."

"I don't think you've fully recovered from your stay at The Institute."

Jake moved to the door. "Probably not," he agreed.

They'd just left the Security Check Section of the docking area and entered the Arriving Passengers Concourse, when Jake said, quietly, "Very unobtrusively, Sid, glance over at the lad in the shuttle attendant uniform to our right."

Gomez rubbed at his new nose. "The *hombre* who emerged from the door marked *Staff Arrivals*?"

"Him, yeah."

"Not an especially amiable-looking chap. Why are we ogling him?"

"I think," said Jake, "I better tail him and find out where he's staying."

"Okay, I'll go check in and start contacting informants for news of Nat," said his partner, frowning. "But who exactly is this *pendejo* and why's he worth tagging?"

"I thought he was still up in the Freezer prison," answered Jake. "But that's Austin Quadrill."

"*Ai*, he was an expert at arranging explosions, wasn't he?"

"I'm betting he still is," said Jake. "Fact, he might be the fellow who sent the Santa Clara Hotel on to glory."

As Jake turned to move away, Gomez said, "Be sure to ask him if he has anything planned for this satellite."

When Wolfe Bosco scowled, a multitude of new wrinkles joined those already crowded together on his lined little face. "What gives, pal?" he inquired of the disguised Gomez. "You act like you're auditioning for *Galactic G-Men*."

The detective, paying him little heed, continued using the bug-detector on the small office. "One can't be too careful about spy devices when one is about to discuss an important vidwall production," he told the wrinkled little talent agent.

From behind his small desk Bosco asked, "You ever do any voice work, pal? I got this hunch I've heard your voice someplace before."

Satisfied there were no eavesdropping gadgets in the room, Gomez dropped the detector into a pocket. "*Sí*, Wolfe, you've often heard the mellow tones of my voice," he told him. "We've been doing business ever since the days when I was a cop down in Greater LA and—"

"Holy Hannah." The little agent slumped. "It's my old nemesis, my jinx. Sid Gomez."

"*Verdad*, but don't go howling my name around."

"Why the fake honker, pal?"

"Disguise."

"What sort of god-awful mess are you in now, Sid? No,

don't tell me, don't impart any details. Just simply take a hike for yourself.''

"Wolfe, besides being one of the great talent agents on or off the planet, you—"

"Great, am I? You, Sid, as well as that carrot-topped Newz, Inc., broad you hang around with—and to whom you are probably slipping the old salami unless I miss my guess—the pair of you are the main contributors to my fall from grace.'' Standing up, Bosco pointed an accusing finger. "I've sunk so low that I have to peddle android talent up on this second-rate satellite and—"

"What a coincidence," cut in the detective. "It's Natalie Dent I've dropped in to talk to you about."

"Amscray," invited the forlorn agent. "Hit the road, check out. That skirt is poison and—"

"A thousand dollars."

"How's that again?"

Gomez moved closer to the desk. "That's the initial fee I'm offering you, Wolfe," he answered. "As I was trying to say—in addition to being a top-seeded agent, you're also a terrific informant. You've helped me on several cases over the years, and soon as I learned you were in residence on the Movie Palace, why, I—"

"Informant? Say rather stool pigeon," said the wrinkled little man. "A Judas."

"A Judas who'll add at least a thousand dollars to his income for today."

"Twelve hundred."

"Too much, Wolfe."

"I won't have anything to do with Natalie Dent unless you can sweeten the—"

"Okay, eleven hundred."

"Split the diff, Sid."

"Eleven-fifty."

Very slowly, very reluctantly, Bosco invited, "Sit down, Sid."

Gomez sat down.

⸺ 36 ⸺

WHEN THE PAIN caught her this time, Yedra Cortez was crossing the main dining room of the club. She lurched, cried out. Her skull felt as though it had suddenly burst into flame and she saw zigzags of intensely bright colored light go circling around her head.

The young woman staggered, dropping to her knees amidst a stand of yellow holographic bamboo. She knelt there, surrounded by ghostly images of the slanting bamboo reeds, bent in on herself.

"*Mierda,*" she muttered through clenched teeth. "*Mierda.*"

She brought up both hands and pulled at her short-cropped dark hair.

"What's wrong, kid?" Trocadero came hurrying over to her, stepping right through a projected banana tree.

"It's my damned head again, Johnny." Her voice was thin, uneven.

"We got to get you to a medic," said the Teklord.

"No, I'll be okay." The hand she reached out to catch hold of his arm was shaking.

219

"It's that gadget in your coco." He helped her to stand, then guided her over to a table and put her in a chair.

"No, it isn't that. Forget it." She was hunched, both elbows on the tabletop.

"Listen, Quadrill is on the vidphone and he wants to talk to you. But if you feel—"

"That bastard is supposed to be up on the satellite by now. Why the hell is—"

"Yeah, he *is* up there. He's calling from the Movie Palace."

"Why's he doing that? He's liable to tip them off."

"The guy claims he's using a tap-proof phone. A special one he cooked up himself."

She straightened. "I better talk to him."

"You up to it, sure?"

"I'm feeling all right now." Yedra slipped a palmphone out of her pocket. "Put that asshole on."

"You're not looking especially well—even for you, dear," said Quadrill. "How are you feeling?"

"You're calling me from the frigging Movie Palace just to ask how I am, Austin?"

"In point of fact, that *is* one of the reasons," he replied. "I wanted to find out how you're enjoying your headaches."

She exhaled sharply. "What the hell do you know about that?"

He smiled thinly. "You're not as bright as you claim to be," he said. "I'm responsible for what you've been experiencing."

"What's that son of a bitch telling you?" asked Trocadero, leaning closer.

"Hello, Johnny," said Quadrill from the little phonescreen. "Stand aside, would you, until I finish with Yedra?"

"Stand aside, my ass. What's the big idea of—"

"Let him speak," cut in the young woman. "Go on, Austin. What's this all about?"

"I've come up with a little device that allows me to manipulate the skull-phone you saw fit to have installed inside your head," continued Quadrill. "Simple little gadget, but it allows me to send you fairly severe spasms of pain whenever I want to."

"We'll get the damn thing removed," said Trocadero. "You're not going to hurt—"

"Come on, Johnny," said Quadrill. "I've taken care of that too. If anybody starts to operate on Yedra's lovely little skull—well, you don't want to try that."

"Listen, you're working for me," said the Teklord, angry. "What the hell you up to?"

"I want to make sure I get paid all I'm owed," he said quietly.

"I always pay off."

"And I'm equally interested in making sure I survive after my job has been successfully completed."

Yedra said, "You're not going to stop this shit until you've collected and gotten away clear?"

"It bothered me when you found my workshop, dear," he told her. "This is to make sure nothing like that happens again."

Trocadero said, "You have my word that nothing is going to—"

"I also have my gadget, Johnny," he said. "Oh, and by the way. I want a bonus for this job up here."

"Why the hell for?" asked Yedra.

"Because somebody was tailing me—I don't know if it's somebody who's working for you or some kind of cop," Quadrill told her. "Pudgy guy, around fifty, with a couple of chins."

"You're the only one we sent up to the Movie Palace, Austin," she assured him.

"This gentleman arrived shortly after I did," said Quadrill, smiling another small, narrow smile. "But I didn't have any trouble eluding him. It meant extra work though, hence extra money."

"Forget about your damn money," said Trocadero. "I don't want Yedra to suffer any more pain from—"

"Lay off, Johnny," she told him. "You win, Austin."

Quadrill held up a small silvery control panel. "Just a little reminder," he said, and touched one of the keys.

"Oh, Jesus!" The young woman bent over, her head nearly hitting the table.

"Start getting my money ready." Quadrill's image left the phonescreen.

The big blonde woman in the dark blue uniform asked Gomez, "Well, which one?"

He shifted slightly in the railcar seat beside her. "The wide-brimmed hat," he said with very little enthusiasm.

"Instead of this cap with the tassel?"

"If you prefer that one," he said, some impatience in his voice, "then go ahead and wear it."

"What I'd appreciate knowing, Mr. Gomez, is *your* preference." She removed the cap with the tassel and replaced it with the wide-brimmed hat.

"My preference, *Señorita* Kording, is that we get rolling through the innards of the satellite, *muy pronto*."

The small railcar was sitting on the narrow left-hand track at the mouth of one of the many long dim-lit tunnels that crisscrossed the interior of the orbiting Movie Palace.

"Since you're bribing me an impressive amount to do this—and I do appreciate Wolfe Bosco's recommending me for the job—I want to make sure there's nothing about my appearance and attire that rubs you the wrong way."

"Okay, wear the cap."

"It's simply that all of us who work in Interior Main-tenance have the option of wearing either the cap or the hat. Which is why I—"

"Okay, wear the hat."

Nodding, Maybelle Kording tugged down on the brim of the hat, rubbed her gloved hands together and started the closed little car. "I've got all the two-way windows blanked so nobody can see inside," she told the detective. "If you stay scrunched low in your seat, we'll be okay."

"*Bueno.*"

The car rolled a hundred yards and then Maybelle stopped it. She slid her left hand out through a narrow flap in her side window, pressed her palm against a glowing panel on the wall. The wall voxbox said, "Cleared, pro-ceed."

Shortly, Gomez inquired, "You're certain that Natalie Dent is being held in a room off Tunnel 30?"

"I confirmed that right after Wolfe Bosco contacted me," she answered.

"You'll be able to get me inside there?"

"Not a problem, Mr. Gomez," assured Maybelle with a positive nod. "Hold on a sec."

The railcar stopped again, and she pressed her palm against another identification panel. "Cleared, proceed."

"All the highest-ranking Interior Maintenance people can get into any of the rooms down here."

"I have to get in and out," he reminded.

"Well, I wouldn't have accepted the bribe, Mr. Gomez, if I wasn't sure I could deliver," she said.

She stopped again, held out her hand.

"Cleared, proceed."

Maybelle said, "Have you known Wolfe Bosco long?"

"Many a year, *sí*."

"The poor man doesn't seem to enjoy his current job."

"*I'm* not enjoying my current job all that much," admitted Gomez, sinking lower in his seat.

— 37 —

MARRINER GLANCED DOWN through the one-way see-through floor as he went striding across the big room, accompanied by Lana Chen and Ramon Rodriguez.

Far below in the huge oval holostage area the towers and pedramps of Manhattan's Times Square section showed. Snaking through the center of the simulated section of the metropolis was a narrow see-through plastiglass tunnel, filled at the moment by more than two hundred tourists moving slowly, single-file, and gawking.

Flying in low between the towering buildings came a half-dozen silvery saucer craft. Crackling crimson beams came shooting from their underbellies. They sliced through the bodies of the civilians who seemed to be running along the ramps seeking shelter. Chunks of the buildings were bitten away, too, and went falling and tumbling.

"Hokum." Marriner stopped, hands on hips, and frowned downward.

"It's one of our most popular attractions." Rodriguez was a glossy, handsome man with considerable dark wavy hair.

"Just watch this bit now." Marriner pointed with his boot toe at a saucer that was landing in the street.

A silvery side door flapped open and a squat greenish creature with a huge top-heavy head and four arms came hopping clear, brandishing several odd-looking lazrifles.

"God-awful," observed Marriner.

"It's supposed," explained Rodriguez, "to be a Martian invader."

"I know what it's supposed to be, Ramon. But it's trite, much too close to the Martians they're using in the Invasion of Greater Los Angeles concession up on New Hollywood."

"Ramon's right, though," Lana said. "People love this one, much more than that crappy simulation on New Hollywood. I think it has to do with the fact that they can see New York City get devastated. Everybody—even rubes up from New York itself—enjoys that."

"It's got to start being more sophisticated." Marriner resumed walking toward a distant doorway.

"I have," admitted Rodriguez, dropping to his hands and knees and staring down as more Martians started disembarking from the saucers, "been seriously thinking about upgrading them."

Marriner asked Lana, "How much does that bitch know?"

"Natalie Dent, after some physical persuasion and a nudge from some powerful biochemicals, confided that she knows one hell of a lot."

Rodriguez had caught up with them. "Somebody is wise to tonight's meeting?"

"Worry about the Martians," advised Marriner. "Go on, Lana."

They entered a twisting, down-slanting hallway. "She got her tip from a fellow associated with Anzelmo's London branch,'' the Chinese woman continued. "I sent his name along to somebody in England."

"How much does Newz, Inc., know?"

"They know that you and Anzelmo and the rest are meeting," she said. "They have a fair idea of what it's all about."

Marriner went rapidly down another curving ramp. "Can we arrange to have them forget about it?"

"I'm already looking into that," said Lana.

He pressed his hand to an ID plate next to a grey door. "What about Dent?"

The door slid silently open and she followed him into a large domed meeting room. "We either have to kill her or do a very effective brainwipe."

Stopping at the head of the big oval meeting table, Marriner rested a fist atop it and leaned forward. "Easier to kill her," he concluded.

After he stepped through the wall, Gomez announced, "I'm wearing a false nose, but it's me, Gomez. The secsystem is turned off for approximately five minutes, Nat. Let's get you loose from that *catedra* and depart for someplace else."

"I can't imagine, with all the noses to pick from, you chose that one." The auburn-haired reporter straightened in the metal chair, straining against her bonds. "Even though you do seem to make a habit of rescuing me from messy scrapes in some of the most unlikely spots, I wasn't expecting you to come save me this time."

Severing the cords that bound her, he said, "Actually, *cara*, Cosmos was hired by your bosses to come fetch you out of this latest mess."

Sidebar came creaking to his feet. "Five minutes isn't that long a time," he pointed out. "Suppose we save the rest of this tearful reunion till we get the hell clear of here.''

''*Bueno*,'' agreed the detective, rubbing at Natalie's legs. ''Think you can navigate yourself over to that opening in yonder wall?''

''You don't have to massage my limbs that high up, Gomez.'' She pulled clear, tried a few hobbling steps in the direction of the wall, and then her legs failed, crumpled.

Gomez lunged and caught her around the waist. ''Excuse this further untoward intimacy, Nat,'' he said, pulling her upright and guiding her toward the escape opening.

''I guess, which isn't all that odd, considering what I've been through in the past few hours, that I'm a little fuzzy in my thinking,'' she told him. ''So forgive me, Gomez, if I sound unusually cranky or—''

''You don't sound *unusually* cranky at all, Nat,'' he assured her.

''I just happened to notice those awful inflamed red marks on my arms,'' she said, holding on to him. ''They must've given me more than one shot then.''

''At least five,'' he said. ''Now, I've hired a railcar for this excursion. The thing's parked right outside and down the ramp.''

''Can we all fit into it?'' asked the cambot as he followed them out through the panel in the wall.

''You and Nat will hunker in the storage area in the back,'' he instructed, helping Natalie to make her way downramp toward the left-hand track.

''Are you going to drive this contraption?'' she asked.

''I hired the driver along with it, a personable *mujer* name of Maybelle Kording.''

When they were less than five feet from the waiting rail-car, the driver's-side door snapped open.

Gomez gave Natalie a hard shove that sent her falling. "Duck, gang," he warned. "That ain't Maybelle in there."

— ≡ 38 ≡ —

It TOOK JAKE two bribes, a threat and nearly two hours of time after he'd lost Austin Quadrill to locate where he was temporarily holed up on the Movie Palace.

"Make that after he ditched me," Jake reminded himself as he made his away along a corridor in Shuttle Crew Dorm 3.

Jake was near certain Quadrill hadn't recognized him. Meaning the demolition man was being careful to ditch anyone who attempted to trail him.

It seemed highly likely that Quadrill was up here to plant some sort of bomb.

In fact, he may have planted it already in the time Jake had wasted trying to locate him again.

"I've got to find the guy damn quick," Jake said. "Before he gets away from this satellite and leaves the whole damn thing to blow up."

He slowed, stopped at the door marked 3/5. He stepped forward to touch the visitor button below the spy hole.

There was no response. The eye in the door wasn't activated.

He gave the button another, more aggressive push.

Nothing happened.

Getting out his lock-picking gadget, Jake set it to match the make of door mechanism and clicked it on.

After a very faint murmur of protest the door whirred, swung open inward.

He drew his stungun out of his shoulder holster and paused, listening, to one side of the now open doorway.

Then he carefully crossed into the small shadowy parlor.

"Damn."

Reaching back, Jake shut the door behind him before walking over to the dead man.

Gomez missed with his first shot.

"*Maldito,*" he observed as the silent beam of his stungun passed an inch to the right of the shoulder of the large, red-cheeked gunman who'd replaced Maybelle in the driveseat of the waiting railcar.

Immediately, even as he was muttering his disappointment, Gomez went rolling along the trackside passway.

The red-faced man lurched out of the compartment, lazgun gripped in both thick hands. He fired at the scooting detective the instant his wide feet slapped down on the passway surface.

The sizzling beam from the lazgun went flashing by a good yard or so to Gomez' left.

But the beam caught the sprawled camera robot, lopping off his left leg a couple inches below the knee.

"Fight back," the crouching Natalie urged the injured bot.

"They disarmed me, if you'll recall."

"Well, at least take some pictures, Sidebar. I can use some good action footage."

Gomez, meantime, had gone dodging in another direction. He flipped to his feet and fired again.

This shot proved considerably more effective.

It hit the red-faced man in the lower rib cage. Doing a half spin, he performed a wobbly curtsy before smacking down flat out.

Gomez leaped over the settling body, taking hold of Natalie's hand. "We're going to have to come up with an alternative escape plan, *chiquita*," he told her while helping her to rise. "Somebody seems to be aware of my advent."

The wobbly reporter was glancing around her. "How far would we be from Tunnel 29?"

Pointing back along the tracks, he answered, "Entrance is back that way about a half-mile. Why?"

Sidebar opened a large compartment in his metallic chest. "I'm supposed to have a spare leg stowed in here someplace," he said, starting to probe inside himself. "Unless they confiscated that too."

"I have a map—purchased for a considerable fee, I might mention—that lays out most of the interior setup aboard the satellite," continued Natalie, letting go of Gomez and attempting to remain standing unaided. She swayed considerably, yet managed to continue upright. "If we can get to Tunnel 29, I may yet be able to complete my assignment."

"You're alluding to getting a scoop about the Marriner/Anzelmo conference?"

Natalie said, "I should've realized that a gumshoe of your proven abilities would've found out about even—"

"Hold it, be quiet for a moment, *bonita*." He left her to ease nearer the parked railcar. "I think I heard something."

"This thing's tarnished badly, but otherwise usable." The cambot stood up, having replaced his damaged leg with the spare he'd been carrying within. "We better be up and doing, folks."

Gomez leaned forward and thrust his upper body in through the open doorway of the car. "*Ay*, it's Maybelle, groaning as she returns to consciousness," he said in the reporter's direction. "Her colleague apparently bopped her on the *cabeza* and stowed her in back prior to attempting to trap us."

Natalie unsteadily made her way over to his side. "Can you trust her?"

"I find that bump on her head to be sufficiently convincing," he answered. "If she's in any shape to run this car, she can get us back through the security checks a lot easier than I can."

Natalie nodded. "Then let's get everybody loaded aboard and get the heck away."

"*Sí, pronto.*"

As Jake walked closer, the small golden kitten that was lying on the carpeting came briefly to life. It took three tottering steps in the direction of the corpse of Austin Quadrill before giving out a tiny, forlorn meow and falling over.

It splashed in the blood and other things that had come spilling out of the dead man when the beam of a lazgun had gone knifing across his lower abdomen.

"What the hell led up to Quadrill's getting knocked off?" Jake asked himself, frowning.

If it was to stop him from planting a bomb, why close him up in his room again and leave the body there?

Taking out a sniffer gadget from his jacket pocket, Jake began exploring the parlor of the small apartment.

A man other than Quadrill had been in here with him a half hour ago.

"Wait now." Jake touched the keypad of the detecting

device. "Yeah, the other lad was in here before Quadrill came back."

Meaning somebody had been waiting there for him.

He crossed over to the small silvery suitcase that sat a few feet from the body.

It lay open, only partially splattered.

There was nothing inside except another tiny clockwork kitten.

Jake knelt beside the case. "This must be what he was carrying his bomb materials in," he reflected. "How the hell, though, did he get anything past their security system up here?"

Except that that was Quadrill's specialty. Yeah, even back when Jake first encountered him, Quadrill had a reputation for being able to slip by just about any kind of security.

"Okay, let's say he smuggled his bomb aboard the Movie Palace and got it planted someplace before he was killed." Jake leaned back against the arm of a rubberoid lounging chair. "So where is it?"

Kneeling again, he ran the gadget over the open suitcase.

There was no trace of a bomb.

Did that mean Quadrill hadn't actually smuggled an explosive device aboard?

Or had he concocted something that was undetectable and untraceable?

"Let's assume he came here with a bomb that can't be spotted," said Jake thoughtfully. "Okay, so I don't follow the bomb—I follow him."

He stood, aimed the sniffer at the carpeting.

"Yeah, Quadrill forgot to make himself untraceable," he said.

He'd be able to follow the trail Quadrill had left earlier,

and that would take Jake right to where the bomb was planted.

"What exactly I'll do after I find the damn thing—well, I'll figure that out later."

With the gadget held in his right hand, he moved to the door.

It opened ten seconds before he reached it, and a slick, handsome man with a lazgun was standing out there in the hall. "Just stay right there, friend," he advised.

NATALIE STUMBLED. "THEY certainly don't keep these supply tunnels very well illuminated," she complained.

Catching her and helping her maintain her balance, Gomez said, "Tourists don't usually stray into this part of the satellite."

They were walking along a catwalk that bordered a gradually ascending ramp. A single track ran along the center of the ramp. Small floating globes every few feet provided a thin yellowish light.

The reporter again brought her pocket talkpad up to her ear to listen to her notes. "We're still going in the—"

"Back, *carita*," warned Gomez, putting his arm in front of the young woman and pushing her back against the tunnel wall.

A string of five monowheel supply carts went rattling and chugging by, loaded down with 'ponic produce.

"Yikes," said the camera robot as the edge of a metal crate protruding over the edge of the last wagon in line scraped at his metal chest. "Wouldn't you know it, more damage to my surface."

"It would really be helpful, and don't think I'm trying to be overly critical, Sidebar, but adopting an attitude of looking on the bright side, would certainly be helpful on a mission like this one we're embarked on, because—"

"What bright side, Nat?" the bot inquired. "Thus far I've been disabled with a stunner, had my favorite leg lopped off, been scraped, scratched and—"

"*Por favor*, let's continue on our way," suggested the detective.

"Oh, and thanks for pulling me out of the way of those overloaded wagons, Gomez."

"*De nada*." He patted her on the backside, urging her to move along.

Natalie frowned over her shoulder at him, but said nothing. She put the talkpad to her ear. Nodding, she dropped it into her pocket and started climbing along the narrow catwalk.

After a few moments, Sidebar remarked, "Lettuce."

Gomez frowned back at him. "Now what?"

"I stepped in some lettuce."

After a few more moments, Natalie listened to her notes again. "Okay," she said. "Around this next bend there's supposed to be some sort of safety ladder. We have to shinny up that for quite a ways and then there's supposed to be an unlocked metal door."

"How far," asked the bot, "is quite a ways, Nat?"

"A thousand feet," she answered. "And forgive me if I give the impression that I'm continually and constantly nagging everybody, but I believe I have, on more than one previous occasion, mentioned that I don't really favor being addressed constantly as Nat. My name is Natalie and, while I don't insist that employees of mine address me any more formally than that—although it wouldn't hurt you, Sidebar, to use the appellation Miss Dent now and then, especially when we're in public situations, why—''

"We're crawling through a sewer basically," put in the robot. "It's not my idea of a public occasion."

"*Vámonos*," prompted Gomez. "Let's keep moving."

"There's the ladder." Natalie hurried along the catwalk to gaze up into the shadows.

Gomez walked over to the base of the metal-rung ladder, reached up to test the lowest rung with his hand. "I'll lead the parade, Miss Dent," he told her, and pulled himself up until his feet were resting on the bottom rung.

Natalie slid her talkpad into her skirt pocket and stretched up both hands. "I'd appreciate a little assistance, Gomez," she said.

He climbed a few rungs higher, twisted and dangled down his right arm. "Catch hold, *chiquita*," he offered.

On her second try she managed to grab his wrist and was lifted up onto the narrow ladder. "Okay, I've got a perch on the darn thing. Thanks."

"Don't worry about me," called the camera bot. "I'll just climb up the wall somehow."

"You're extraordinarily dexterous," Natalie reminded him from above. "After all, being able to cover every sort of news story, to shoot, really, vidfootage that's almost always, at the very least, passable, you have to be able to get yourself into all sorts of odd and unusual places and positions. So catching hold of a simple little ladder ought not to present too much of a challenge."

"I didn't imply it was a challenge," answered Sidebar.

Gomez pointed a thumb at the darkness above. "I'll meet you guys upstairs," he said, and commenced climbing.

Clearing his throat, Marriner rose at the head of the large oval plastiglass meeting table. He glanced around at the eleven other places and asked, "Where's Maurice Pettifaux?"

Lana Chen, clad in a crisp off-white lab coat and seated next to him, said, "An accident, so I'm told, prevents his attending."

"What sort of accident?"

Anzelmo, at the opposite end of the table, answered, "Maurice got himself ambushed in a goddamned quaint little alley in the Left Bank Enclave in Paris."

The plump, crimson-haired Mrs. Dooley said, "They used at least a half-dozen lazrifles on poor Maury."

"Yeah," confirmed Anzelmo. "The frog cops never were able to find all of him."

From midtable Roger Giford said, "This sounds like a reprisal to me, Marriner."

"Exactly," added Mrs. Dooley. "Our less fortunate Tek brothers getting back at us because they've heard we're throwing in with you."

"Nobody," Marriner assured them, "nobody whatsoever knows anything of this plan."

"Oh, yeah? Then what about . . ." Anzelmo began patting his various pockets with his gnarled hands. "What the frig is that name?" The old Teklord kept frisking himself until he located, in an inner coat pocket, a small yellow faxmemo. "Okay, here it is. What about Natalie Dent?"

"A minor nuisance," said Marriner. "Nothing more. Certainly not anyone to worry about."

Anzelmo leaned forward, both elbows smacking the tabletop. "Does she happen to be aboard this flapping satellite now?"

Marriner held up his hand in a keep-calm gesture. "Natalie Dent was apprehended soon after she arrived on the Movie Palace," he told the angry Teklord. "She's not going to tell anyone anything. Not ever."

Mrs. Dooley frowned deeply. "That's the broad who works for Newz, Inc., isn't it? Always poking her nose into things."

"That sure as hell is who we're talking about," said Anzelmo. "Are you trying to con us, Marriner, into believing that her bosses at Newz don't have a fricking idea why she came up here?"

"The few people at Newz who have any hint of this are being neutralized," Marriner said. "Trust me. As for Natalie Dent herself, we have her safely locked away. After this meeting, steps will be taken to . . ." He'd become aware that Lana was tugging on his sleeve. Leaning down closer, he asked her, "What?"

Lana put her lips close to his ear to whisper, "Just before I came in I learned she's not in her room anymore."

"Then where the hell is she?"

"We don't know, but she's being hunted," replied Lana. "Change the subject, Leon."

He straightened up. "Now that we've got this minor stuff out of the way," he said, "we can move to the real business of this meeting. My gifted colleague Lana Chen will give you a demonstration of the just perfected TekNet system."

—≡ 40 ≡—

JAKE LOOKED FROM the lazgun to the face of the handsome man who stood pointing it at him, and grinned. "Ramon Rodriguez," he said, recognizing him. "This looks like a step up for you from being assistant manager at the Boardwalk Teenage Android Bordello down in the San Pedro Sector of Greater LA."

"Do I know you?"

"Under these false trappings I'm Jake Cardigan."

Rodriguez took a surprised step backwards. "When I got the call about trouble down here," he said, "I didn't expect to find Jake Cardigan, ex-con turned private eye."

"You've found a hell of a lot more than that, Ramon," Jake told him. "Take a look inside while I get on the track of—"

"You're not going much of anyplace, Cardigan." He made a shooing motion with his gun hand. "Back inside so I can have a look around. I understand something pretty serious took place in this joint."

Jake preceded him back into the room. "You must know this lad," he said, stepping aside and nodding toward the

243

sprawled corpse. "There's a strong possibility that—"

"Holy Christ, is that—what the hell is his name?— Quadrill? Yeah, Austin Quadrill."

"That's exactly who it is, yeah," confirmed Jake. "I'm near certain he brought a bomb aboard."

Rodriguez took a few reluctant steps nearer the body. "I never can get used to the smell," he admitted. "What's that about a bomb?"

"It's Quadrill's specialty, sneaking explosives into—"

"Naw, he couldn't have," insisted Rodriguez. "We got too good a secsystem. Hell, I supervise that myself."

"Even so, Ramon"—Jake jerked a thumb in the direction of the corpse—"the odds are Quadrill was hired to take care of Marriner and—"

"What are you talking about, Cardigan? Marriner's nowhere near the Movie Palace."

"It was most likely Johnny Trocadero who hired Quadrill to take care of everybody attending Marriner's meeting with Anzelmo and company tonight."

"You're not supposed to know about that."

"Point is, I do," Jake said. "I also know Quadrill was scheduled to take off from the Movie Palace just under three hours from now. That means his bomb can go off anytime after that."

"This is all bullshit," said Rodriguez. "You more than likely killed this poor bastard and now you're trying to con me with some—"

"Three hours isn't an especially long stretch of time, Ramon," he cut in. "I think I can backtrack along Quadrill's trail and find out where he stowed the bomb. After that we're going to have to—"

"No, what you're going to have to do is get your ass into a detention area until I can—Oof!"

Not betraying his intention, Jake had all at once feinted

to the right and then sidestepped and kicked out at Rodriguez. His boot took the surprised man in the crotch and he howled.

Jake dived forward, caught the gun arm and snapped it down.

The lazgun went off and dug a deep smoky zigzag rut across nearly two square feet of carpeting.

A fire warning alarm started hooting.

Two punches to the already groggy Rodriguez' chin and the handsome man lost consciousness. He stayed upright for about ten seconds before falling over and landing flat out next to the dead man.

Skirting the newly splashed blood, Jake headed for the way out.

Yedra Cortez was walking along the oceanside when twilight started to arrive.

Gulls, dark shadows across the greying sky, came gliding in low over the sea to land on the damp sand.

They began to look strange to the young woman, distorted. With immense wings and thin elongated bodies, and all of them colored a pulsing, glittering black.

A moment later the pain exploded in her head again. It was worse this time, throbbing in her skull and then shooting through her body. A cry came spilling out of her and she fell, knees jabbing hard into the darkening sand.

The gulls cried out like giant crows as they changed colors and started to wheel and whirl overhead, circling ever closer to her. They changed colors, too. Crimson, gold, dead white, silver, yellow, crimson, gold.

Then they went swirling away and night suddenly hit. She was aware of nothing but the pain.

Gasping, whimpering, she yanked her palmphone out of her trouser pocket. Yedra had to bring the damn thing right up to her eyes to see it. Bracing herself against the pain, she managed to punch out a number.

The phone couldn't have taken as long to answer as she thought it did.

Finally the face of a tired-looking, pale man showed on the tiny screen. "Jesus, Yedra, what the hell's wrong with you?"

"Nick?"

"Yeah, it's me. Where are you? I'll send somebody to—"

"I'm okay. Okay," she said. "I thought you. Told me that the guy you sent up. To the Movie Palace to take. Care of Quadrill and. Kill him soon as the bomb. Was planted succeeded?"

"I did, honey. He took care of it for you, just like you asked me."

"But the damned. Gadget that Quadrill had and. Was using to give me these. Damned headaches, you said he got. That and was bringing it back here. Nick."

"He did get what you wanted, Yedra, right after he took care of the guy," said Nick, concern showing on his pale face. "The trouble is . . ."

"What? Tell me."

"He can't seem to figure out how it works exactly. You know, how to turn it off like you said to do."

"I saw Quadrill. Use it. Nick. It's on now. Giving me a lot of pain."

"I know, I'm sorry, honey," apologized Nick. "But my guy was calling me from the shuttle on his way home here. Maybe, you know, it could be I didn't hear him all that good."

"When's he. Going to be in GLA. Nick? He's got to bring it to. Me so I can stop. These goddamn headaches."

"Listen, Yedra. Tell me where you are."

"At the beach. Because I like to walk. Along here."

"Where, honey, which beach?"

"By Johnny's new club."

"I'll contact Johnny and tell him to come down there and get you. Can you hold on?"

The pain took her over and she couldn't talk anymore.

—≡41≡—

ANZELMO PUSHED BACK in his chair. "Go over that again, lady," he requested of Lana Chen.

"All right, this disc is the only headgear our customers will need." She was standing at the front of the meeting room with a small grey disc held between thumb and forefinger. "This'll give you a better look at it."

Lana placed the disc on a small projection stage, and a large holographic image of it formed over the center of the meeting table.

Mrs. Dooley, frowning and with her head cocked to the right, studied the projection. "What about the Brainbox every Tekkie has to hook the headgear to?"

"We've succeeded in making that superfluous," put in Marriner, smiling.

Lana continued, "You'll notice a tiny clip at the back of the disc. That allows you to—"

"Where?" asked Macri. "I don't see any—"

"That little silvery dingus, schmuck," said Anzelmo, pointing at the floating hologram.

"Oh, yeah, there it is."

"You attach the disc to your hair," explained Lana, placing the demonstration disc over her ear, "and that provides sufficient contact with your brain."

Mrs. Dooley asked, "And, I believe you told us earlier, there are no Tek chips needed either?"

"They're no longer necessary," answered Marriner, his smile broadening.

"I came into this project late," said Macri, "and I guess I'm not too bright in some areas. But it seems to me that this is going to put Tek cartels like mine out of business."

"It puts," Giford corrected, "our major competitors out of business, old man."

On a small table next to the projection stage rested a small portable computer. "From now on," said Lana, moving closer to it, "anyone who has access to one of these can have access to Tek."

"So long as," added Marriner, "they deal with our consortium."

Anzelmo turned his chair to get a better view, resting one hand on his knee. "How does that headgear connect with the computer?"

"Anytime you're within five feet of a terminal, you can become connected," answered the Chinese woman. "You activate the whole operation verbally, reciting a series of passcodes and then ordering whatever kind of Tek illusion you want to enjoy."

Macri was frowning. "I don't quite comprehend how the money gets from them to us," he admitted. "Can you, slow, explain exactly—"

"Emergency! Security emergency!" announced the trio of voxboxes floating up near the ceiling.

Marriner jumped up, glancing at Lana. "Any idea what the hell is—"

"Rodriguez is on his way here," she replied, tapping at

the voxbug in her left ear. "He says—No, I'm losing him."

A different voice from a different voxbox said, "Ramon Rodriguez requesting entry."

Anzelmo pushed back farther in his chair and, with considerable effort, stood up. "You promised us complete security for this meeting, Marriner," he said, upset. "But instead we get bitches from Newz and now—"

"Rodriguez can enter," said Marriner toward the ceiling.

A wall panel slid aside and the slick, handsome man came hurrying in. He moved to Marriner's side and reported in a low voice, "There may be some kind of bomb aboard the Movie Palace."

"May be—or is?"

"Well, we better assume there is."

"And how the hell did it get past our security checks?"

"I don't know that yet," admitted Rodriguez. "But I think we better assume it is here—because Austin Quadrill has a reputation for being able to plant a bomb just about anywhere."

"Austin Quadrill?" said Anzelmo, shuffling over to them. "Is that son of a bitch here?"

"Well, he is—he was," answered Rodriguez.

"Which is it, asshole?"

Rodriguez took a deep breath before answering, "He got aboard somehow and we think he planted a bomb before he was killed."

"Shit," said Marriner, taking hold of the handsome man by both shoulders. "What the hell are you telling me now?"

"It's a sort of screwed up chain of events," he admitted, and ran his tongue over his upper lip. "Jake Cardigan is on the Movie Palace, too, and it's his notion that—"

"That's wonderful," said Anzelmo, dropping both hands to his sides. "We got a flapping mad bomber who does most of his work for my bitter enemies—assholes like Johnny Trocadero and—''

"That's who Cardigan suspects is behind this whole mess," offered the uneasy Rodriguez.

"And as the frosting on the whole mess," the old Teklord went on, "we got operatives from the frigging Cosmos Detective Agency crawling all over the damn satellite."

Marriner let go of Rodriguez and stood back. "I want to talk to Cardigan," he said quietly.

"We have to find him first," answered Rodriguez even more quietly.

"You had a nice little chat with the bastard," suggested Marriner, "then let him go on about his business."

"He says he can find the bomb Quadrill planted," explained Rodriguez. "And we only have about two and a half hours to—"

"Why did you let him get away from you?" said Marriner. "We've got our own bomb experts. I don't need—"

"I didn't have that much choice. He knocked me flat on my ass and when I awoke—he wasn't there."

Mrs. Dooley had joined them. "Forget about Cardigan," she told them. "What are your people doing about this bomb?"

"I've alerted the entire security force," answered Rodriguez, and licked his lip again. "They're combing every nook and cranny of the entire satellite looking for the explosive device."

"Tell them also," said Marriner, "to look for Cardigan."

— 42 —

IT WAS RODRIGUEZ who found Jake.

Not much of an accomplishment, since all he had to do was walk around the bend in a corridor down near the center of the orbiting satellite and there was Jake.

Grinning, striding right toward him.

"You'll have to come with me, Cardigan," he ordered, pointing his lazgun. "Marriner wants to see you."

"I wouldn't mind seeing *him*," said Jake.

Rodriguez noticed the small grey metal box in Jake's right hand. "Is that it?"

"It is, yeah."

Rodriguez ran his tongue over his upper lip and then his lower lip while he moved, rapidly, over against the strutted metal wall of the corridor. "What's the . . . What's the status of the damn thing, for Christ sake?"

"I inactivated it."

"You know how to do stuff like that, Cardigan? What I mean is, you're sure it won't explode anymore?"

"Oh, it'll explode again," said Jake. "I learned a hell of a lot about bombs while I was with the SoCal State

Police, Ramon. Quadrill was a pretty clever lad, but there's almost no bomb that can't be controlled.''

"Oughtn't you to hand it over to me now? Then I can have our demolition experts make absolutely—"

"Here's how things work," said Jake, speaking slowly and patiently. "Unless Marriner guarantees me and certain friends of mine safe passage off the Movie Palace—I'll rig this to blow again."

"That would be suicide for you," said Rodriguez. "And you'd also kill off hundreds of innocent people."

"So?"

"C'mon, Cardigan, you're not that—"

"Think about it, Ramon," he said evenly. "The Teklords framed me and got me sent up to the Freezer for four years. Four years in suspended animation and when I came out I didn't have a wife anymore and pretty nearly lost my son, too. Sure, I'd like to stay alive—but if I can't, then let's get rid of Anzelmo and his buddies *and* your boss Marriner."

"You're bluffing."

"Better see what Marriner has to say."

After a moment, Rodriguez nodded his sleek head. "Okay, we'll go talk to him."

"You're bluffing, Cardigan," accused Marriner.

"Sure he is," seconded Anzelmo, who was back sitting in his meeting room chair, breathing slowly and with a considerable wheeze.

"I'm not sure of that," said Mrs. Dooley. "I've heard a lot about Cardigan and he's supposed to be mean and—well, not exactly rational."

"That's a good appraisal of my character," said Jake, grinning over at her. "Now, bring Natalie Dent here and then I'll get in touch with my partner, Sid Gomez, and we'll—"

"Don't do anything irrational, Cardigan," said Rodriguez, holding out a placating hand to him and eyeing the little grey box. "But, see, we're going to have a problem here. We sort of lost track of the Dent woman and—"

"Well, I suppose this is as good a dramatic spot as any to make an entrance, although, if you want the absolute truth, I don't go in for flamboyant behavior," said Natalie. A panel in the meeting room wall slid open and she stepped into the big room, followed by Gomez and the camera bot.

Sid gave his partner a lazy salute. "We've been eavesdropping for a spell, *amigo*," he announced.

"Got some terrific footage on the meeting," added Sidebar, tapping his chest.

"That's too bad," said Marriner. "We're going to have to call Cardigan's bluff—and we're going to have to get rid of every damned one of you."

"That really is, and I hope you'll forgive my using a cliché, since I'm known throughout the world, and even in pestholes like this, for my clever and original turns of phrase, mostly academic," said Natalie, folding her arms under her breasts. "You see, the truth of the matter is that it really doesn't matter if—"

"In the name of God," said Anzelmo, "get to the flapping point, lady."

The reporter scowled at him for a few seconds. Then she said, "Okay, all right, we'll do it your way, Mr. Anzelmo. For the past twenty-six minutes your little gathering has been going out to each and every Newz, Inc., client on Earth. So in every major city of this giddy globe, and in every little hamlet and rural village, in the caves beneath the ground and in the deep dark jungles—the few that are left—people now know what you've been up to and what you were plotting. Before the day is too much older, I'd imagine you'll all, each and every one of you, be up to your, if you'll pardon my indelicate expression, fannies in law enforcement agents.''

Anzelmo narrowed his left eye and glared at Marriner. ''You asshole,'' he remarked.

''I agree completely,'' said Marriner, and sat down.

—≣ 43 ≣—

Bascom said, "I'm pleased."

From the chair he was straddling, Jake asked, "Pleased enough to okay that bonus you mentioned earlier?"

"Sure," said the chief of the Cosmos Detective Agency. "I put in for that before Natalie Dent's special Newz broadcast from up there"—he jabbed a thumb in the direction of the ceiling—"had been on the air for more than a few minutes." He turned to gaze in Gomez' direction.

He was standing by one of the high, wide viewwindows, watching dusk settle down.

"Sid, I just alluded to your bonus?"

"I heard. *Gracias.*"

"I was expecting a mite more enthusiasm."

Gomez came away from the window and leaned against one of the worktables. "I'm wondering about some of the loose ends in this case."

"Such as?"

"What about Jill's husband, Ernst Reinman?"

"Paid us the handsome fee he agreed to pay if we found his missing wife," answered Bascom.

"He's tangled up in this whole mess. He could end up in the hoosegow himself."

Bascom said, "The fee agreed upon moved from his account to ours. I have no further interest in the fellow."

"I imagine the police do."

"That's true, Sid," agreed Bascom.

Gomez said, "Does anybody know who killed Austin Quadrill?"

"Somebody hired by the late Yedra Cortez," said the agency chief. "Lieutenant Drexler is on his trail even as we speak."

Gomez frowned. "Late? Is that nasty *mujer* dead and done for?"

"She had a very strange accident," Bascom told them. "Part of her skull exploded."

Jake said, "Quadrill no doubt. Something he arranged before she had him done in."

"I'm glad I'm not on the other side of the fence," said Bascom, leaning back in his desk chair. "Over there you can't trust anybody."

Gomez eased over toward the door. "What say we take our leave, Jake?"

"If that's okay with our employer." Jake was untangling himself from the chair.

"Be off, lads," Bascom said, waving in the direction of the doorway.

Gomez was perched on the deck rail at Jake's beachside condo, his back to the foggy night Pacific. "*Sí* the handsome bonus Bascom is promising to bestow on us for our work on the TekNet case will be gratifying," he admitted.

"But?" Jake, a mug of sincaf held in his left hand, was sitting in a deck chair.

"The prospect of additional wealth, at the moment, fails

to cheer me," he said. "Even the fact that, because of Natalie's worldwide blathering by way of Newz, I am once again, momentarily, a famous and celebrated sleuth doesn't do much to cheer my heart, *amigo*."

Jake took a sip of his sincaf. "The aging process sours some people," he suggested. "Fortunately, I've been able to remain my cheerful self over the years, but you, Sid, seem to—"

"Oh, *verdad*, everybody has taken to calling you Jolly Jake."

Jake leaned forward. "You still brooding about Jill's part in all this?"

"I shouldn't be," he said. "We parted a long time ago."

"But you are?"

Gomez glanced back over his shoulder at the misty ocean. "That's probably part of why I'm feeling glum, yeah," he said. "You probably don't remember when I first met her—but, *Dios*, she was very special to me, Jake. I really believed that . . ." He shrugged one shoulder. "I guess I wasn't nearly as perceptive as I should've been. You'd think a world-famous detective would've tumbled to the fact his wife was . . . well, what she was."

"Still, the same thing—"

The deck vidphone buzzed.

Jake asked, "What?"

"Important call for Mr. Gomez."

"Who?"

"Jill Bernardino."

Jake looked over at his partner.

Gomez nodded. "I'll take it." He left the rail and picked up the phone. "Gomez *aquí*."

"Sid, I hope I'm not interrupting anything too important." His onetime wife's image was on the tiny phonescreen. "But when I heard you were over there, I figured Jake wouldn't mind if—"

"It's okay. But hold on a minute, *chiquita*." After nodding at Jake, he carried the phone off the deck and a dozen or so yards along the beach. "*Sí*, what's happening, Jill?"

"I've been making some decisions," she told him. "I'll be leaving this hideaway that Bascom arranged for me in a couple more days. But I don't want to go back to my husband."

"That's probably a good idea."

She asked, "Ernst was involved in all this mess, wasn't he?"

"There's a strong possibility he was."

"He did set me up with Johnny Trocadero, didn't he?"

Gomez stopped just out of reach of the foamy surf and gazed seaward finally. "We didn't really go into that too much, Jill," he answered finally. "But there's a damned good chance that Lieutenant Drexler and the SoCal State cops are going to keep poking around."

She asked, "Would you, working as an official Cosmos Agency operative, dig into it for me? When I divorce Ernst, I want to have every bit of damaging—"

"Jill," he interrupted. "No, I won't be able to handle that for you."

"But you—"

"I came and saved you when you were in trouble, *sí*, I know," he told her. "But that's all I can do for you, *cara*. I won't be part of your life anymore."

After a long silence, she said, "Yes, I see." And then: "Good-bye, Sid."

"*Adiós.*"

Climbing back on the deck, Gomez returned the phone. Jake asked, "Something?"

"Nothing," he answered, and turned away.